A Death in Devon

Sugar Martin Vintage Cozy
Mysteries – Book One

Shéa MacLeod

Sunwalker Press

A Death in Devon
Sugar Martin Vintage Cozy Mysteries – Book One
COPYRIGHT © 2019 by Shéa MacLeod
All rights reserved.
Printed in the United States of America.

Cover Art by Mariah Sinclair/mariahsinclair.com
Editing by Alin Silverwood

The characters and events portrayed in this book are fictitious. Any similarity to real persons, living or dead, is coincidental and not intended by the author.

No part of this book may be reproduced, or stored in a retrieval system, or transmitted in any form or by any means, electronic, mechanical, photocopying, recording, or otherwise, without express written permission of the publisher.

Acknowledgements

With thanks to Zack and Kyle of the Westgate Bourbon Bar and Taphouse who kept me in vintage cocktails. The sacrifices I make for research!

A big shout out to fellow cozy author, vintage lover, and afternoon tea aficionado, C Morgan Kennedy, who let me bounce ideas off her and never got tired of talking about cozies.

Dedication

To Linda
who loves a fabulous adventure.

Chapter 1

When that letter arrived, I should have known that whoever sent it was up to no good. It had the smell of devilry around it, above and beyond the fact it came from a solicitor's office. But when an envelope arrives with a stamp from London, England, a person can hardly refuse it. Which is how I found myself in my current pickle, staring down the barrel of a dueling pistol.

But I'm jumping ahead of myself. Let me back up a bit to the day I received the letter.

It was a grim and gloomy day—as spring days often are in Portland—and I'd decided to wile it away in my pajamas, reading a detective novel (Erle Stanley Gardner's *The Case of the Lonely Heiress*, if you must know.) when I should have been looking for a new job. When the postman rang the bell to have me sign for the letter, we'd both gotten a shock. Him, because it was two in the afternoon and I looked like I'd just crawled out of bed, and me... well, letters from solicitors are rarely welcomed.

I stared at the missive in my hand, trying desperately to regather my wits. I'm not usually a witless person, but the missive had rendered me speechless.

The paper was thick, creamy vellum and must have cost a pretty penny. The typing was neat and precise—not at all like my machine which had a faded ribbon and a chipped letter "A." The signature at the bottom was written in swirling black ink. And don't get me started on the red-waxed seal on the envelope. It was definitely not the sort of letter people in Portland, Oregon—population 15,000—got every day.

I read it again, perhaps for the twenty-seventh time:

> *Dr. Miss Martin,*
> *We are sorry to inform*
> *you that your aunt, Miss*

> *Euphegenia Graves, has recently passed.*

The surname was unfamiliar to me, nor was I aware I had an aunt. I mean, yes, I had aunts. Most people do. Six of them, in fact, but this particular aunt was one I'd never heard of.

> *Miss Graves has left you an inheritance.*

Visions of dollar bills floated through my mind. I could really use a bit of money. My last secretarial job had paid poorly and ended abruptly (I may or may not have punched a fellow employee in the jaw. Don't worry. He deserved it). I'd been unable to find work in the last four months. If I didn't find something soon, my savings would be gone.

> *Enclosed is an airline ticket in your name. You must claim your inheritance in person.*

There was a bunch of legal jargon, followed by the signature.

Regards,
James Woodward,
Solicitor
Woodward & Woodward
Solicitors
London, England

I picked up the ticket again. Sure enough, it was a flight to London leaving on the following Monday. I sat back, stunned. Miss Euphegenia Graves had left me money. Money I was flying to England to collect. England! I'd never even been out of the state of Oregon before, never mind the country. And on a plane, too!

The thought sent a shiver of excitement mixed with fear down my spine. Once upon a time, I'd dreamt of traveling the world. But then the war had come and, well, we all have to make sacrifices, don't we?

But who was Euphegenia Graves?

There was only one person to ask. My mother. She loved keeping up on all the family gossip. Who'd married who. Who had how many children. Where those children went to college, and so on. Plus, all the scandals. Like the time her cousin, Barbara Jean, had an affair with the postman—or was it the milk man?—and nine months later had a little girl who didn't look at all like her husband, Larry.

Padding to my bedroom, I quickly changed into a simple blue dress with cap sleeves and an A-line skirt, and swept my dark hair into a an updo. Tucking the letter into my purse, I donned my blue trench coat (which was perhaps three or four years out of fashion), a matching Tam (a recent indulgence mere moments before losing my job), and gloves. It was a short walk from the cute little red brick apartment building where I lived to my parents Craftsman—which was fortunate, as I didn't own a car. I was glad they hadn't moved out to the suburbs yet, although my mother kept pushing. She loved the idea of one of those modern ranch homes they were building out near Milwaukie.

It was early May 1948, with the slightest chill in the air. It was blustery and overcast, but I figured if it rained, I could dash between the drops. I set out at a brisk walk, low sensible heels making that lovely clacking sound on the pavement, signaling to the world I meant business.

A zippy little tune spun in my mind. Dinah Shore singing "Buttons and Bows." It was high on the charts, and I found it very uplifting. Overcome with energy, I made a little skip.

A pudgy woman walking a pudgy dog sniffed at me. Women my age—closer to thirty than I'd like to admit—did not skip. Well, they did now. I smiled at the dog, gave the woman an arch look, and skipped again. She hustled across the street as if my good mood might be contagious.

At last I arrived at my parents' home and clattered up the steps. I didn't bother to knock; I simply walked in calling out, "Mama, I'm here!"

"In the kitchen, dear," her voice floated back.

I hung my coat on the coat rack next to the front door, removed my hat using the antique mirror that hung next to it, and placed it and my gloves and handbag on the console table just inside the living room.

In the kitchen, Mama was hunched over the table, rolling out pie dough with the rolling pin that had come over with my family on the Oregon Trail. Or at least that's what Mama claimed. She wore a frilly apron over her pale-yellow housedress, and her gray streaked hair was done up in an old-fashioned bun.

"Hi, Mama. Where's Dad?" I swiped a strawberry from the yellow mixing bowl on the table. Mama did love yellow.

"In the garage."

My parents lived in a mock Tudor on the corner of 79th and Fremont. When it was built in 1920, they'd put up a long, skinny building alongside it, connected to the main house by a breezeway. The front of the building nearest the street was a single car garage with creaking great doors that swung open only with a great deal of effort. The back half was a workshop with doors on either side, one leading out to the vegetable garden and the other leading into the walled-in backyard. My father spent most of his time out there in the workshop alternately tinkering with tools and making creative use of the English language when things didn't go his way.

I leaned down to kiss Mama's cheek—I was only five foot four, but she was a good six inches shorter, though we had the same build, curvy rather than willowy—leaving a bright red smudge of lipstick behind. I swiped a bit of flour from her chin. She smelled of cinnamon, sugar, and vanilla, and perhaps a little coffee. Mama did love her coffee.

"Hello, dear," she said, "percolator's on."

"Oh, good." I helped myself to coffee, cream, and sugar. There was always plenty of each at my parents'. Dad always said America was fueled by the stuff.

"Find anything yet?" She meant a job. Or possibly a man. She wasn't particular.

I sighed and sat down at the table. "Unfortunately, no. Linda tried to get me on at her company, but a man applied for the same position."

Mama made a non-committal sound. I knew what she was thinking. *If only Sam hadn't died.*

But Sam had died in the same war that took so many other young men. If he hadn't died, we'd probably be married by now with half a dozen kids, and I wouldn't be worrying about finding a job. But of course Mama would never say any of that despite desperately wanting those grandchildren, and frankly, I didn't see the point in focusing on "what ifs."

As for grandchildren, she already had six of them between my two brothers. Six more was just plain greedy.

"Have you ever heard of a Euphegenia Graves?" I asked over the rim of my coffee mug.

A slight frown line marred her forehead as she focused on placing the crust just so in the pie pan. "I believe your grandmother had an aunt named Euphegenia. Her mother's younger half-sister. Why?"

"This came for me today." I held up the letter.

She dusted her hands free of flour and took the letter gingerly. Fishing a pair of round-rimmed glasses out of the pocket of her apron, she slid them on and read. "Well, my heavens."

I took back the letter. "So, she *is* related to us?"

"Oh, yes, it has to be your great-great aunt. Euphegenia is a family name, as you well know."

I did, to my eternal sorrow. My maternal grandmother's name had also been Euphegenia, and I'd been named for her. Except no one in the world, not even my mother, called me Euphegenia.

Up until I was six, everyone had simply called me Eugie—which is nearly as bad. And then one day, it may have been my sixth birthday now I think on it, my father scooped me up in his burly arms and declared, "You are sweet as sugar!" And it stuck. From that day to this, everyone who doesn't want a fist in their kisser has called me Sugar.

Perhaps it seems odd that a woman of some twenty-eight years would prefer to be called Sugar, but wouldn't you if you were saddled with a name like Euphegenia? I rest my case.

"Are you going?" my mother asked, handing me back the letter and returning to her pie crust.

"I don't see why not. It should be an adventure." The very idea set my blood singing. Things had been so dull for so long I was in dire need of a good adventure.

"Be careful," she pleaded.

"Mama, it's England, not Timbuktu," I assured her, refilling my mug. "They're quite civilized."

"I don't want them taking advantage of you," she insisted. "A young girl all alone in a foreign country. And they were very badly damaged by the war, or so I hear."

"I'm hardly a young girl, and I know how to take care of myself. I worked in the shipyards during the war, if you recall."

"Not at all a suitable job for a young woman," she lamented.

"No indeed," I agreed, although I'd enjoyed the job thoroughly. I'd made an excellent welder. So excellent that my supervisor had told me on the sly that I was better than any man he'd ever worked with. Not that that stopped them from paying me half what they'd pay a man, then letting me go once the men came back from the war. I was less excellent at the whole secretary thing. "But I had my duty to country, didn't I?"

"And you performed it magnificently!" she said stoutly as she slid the pie into the oven. She paused thoughtfully. "You know, Sugar, they don't drink coffee in England. They drink *tea*." She said "tea" like it was a four-letter word instead of three. Mama was serious about her morning beverage. "What will you *do*?"

"When in Rome, I suppose."

"But you won't be in Rome."

I very nearly rolled my eyes. "Of course, not Mama."

"If you were in Rome, there'd be coffee."

"It'll be a quick trip," I assured her, rising to kiss her on the cheek before rinsing out my cup. "I'll be there and back so fast you'll hardly know I'm gone."

It was difficult to decide what to pack, but in the end, I figured I wouldn't be gone terribly long. A week perhaps. Two at most.

I suppose it was fortunate I didn't have a particularly big wardrobe. I'd a nice green victory suit which I used for interviews. Neatly pressed with freshly ironed ruffle collar and a new hat, it would be perfect for travelling. A couple of dresses, a skirt, a pair of slacks—one never knew when those would come in handy—and a few blouses and cardigans, plus a spring trench coat was about all I'd need for such a short trip. Add the requisite number of hats, shoes, accessories, and toiletries, and my father was mumbling to himself about women's baggage being the reason the *Titanic* sank.

I ignored his mutterings as was expected, gave him a peck on the cheek and a thank you for driving me to the airport, and flagged down a sky hop to help with my luggage.

I was feeling very glamorous and sophisticated as I strode through the airport with my handbag on one arm, and a new book by Agatha Christie, *There is a Tide*, in the other hand. I couldn't wait to read it.

My heart thumped wildly in my chest as I waited at the gate with the other passengers, all dressed to the nines. The men wore suits and ties, and the women their best Sunday dresses and brand-new hats. I myself had overindulged in an adorable little green pillbox to match my suit. I might have been broke, but that didn't mean I had to look it.

At last they let us climb the mobile stairway and board the great, shining metal bird. I was shown to a comfortable seat by a uniformed stewardess who offered me a selection of magazines to read. I politely refused, intending instead to spend my time reading my new book.

I managed to get a few chapters in between gaping at the landscape rushing by beneath us, but after switching airplanes in New York, the exhaustion of too much excitement and not enough sleep finally overwhelmed me and I nodded off. I only woke when the stewardess nudged me.

"We're approaching London, Miss."

I thanked her and closed my eyes before turning my head toward the window. This was it. The moment all my dreams of international travel came true.

I opened my eyed and gasped in delight. The whole of London spread out beneath me like something out of a movie, from the Thames snaking its way through the city, to the tall clock tower which housed Big Ben. As we drew ever nearer, I could make out the tiny little boats sailing back and forth under London Bridge. And was that? It must be! St. Paul's Cathedral.

My stomach quivered with excitement. For the first time in the whole of my life, I was about to step foot on foreign soil. I could hardly wait!

If only I'd known what was to come.

Chapter 2

Included with my airline ticket had been directions to the hotel where the solicitor, Mr. Woodward, had arranged for me to stay the duration of my trip. He'd assured me that everything was "sorted," which I took to mean things had been worked out, and that I didn't have to pay a dime. This was a relief, since I didn't have much in the way of dimes currently. I assumed that would be remedied shortly, but golly, it was nice to know I didn't have to find a place on my own.

Another sky hop, this one with a charming English accent, helped me to the curb with my luggage and flagged down a black cab. Soon I was bundled into the back and swooping through the streets of London like any seasoned traveler. I was positively giddy!

The city was an odd juxtaposition of gorgeous Victorian or Art Deco buildings perched next to piles of rubble or bombed out husks. Meanwhile, new construction was springing up where the ruins had been cleared away, and older structures which could be salvaged were swarming with scaffolding and workmen.

The grounds of Hyde Park (I knew it was Hyde Park because the driver told me so.) had finally been returned to lawn after years of use as Victory Gardens to feed the populace during the war. Shop windows showed off the new fuller-skirted fashions now that the rationing of fabric had eased. Window boxes were filled with flowers instead of vegetables. It would take some time yet, but London was returning to its old self. The self I'd dreamed about since I'd borrowed a travel book from the library when I was seventeen.

At last we pulled up in front of a white stone building with a charming little portico and pillars—also white—and a tiny porch tiled in black and white squares. The door was black with a glass insert and, as soon as the cabbie helped me out of the car, it swung open, and a uniformed bellhop appeared to assist with the luggage.

"Hullo," the freckle-faced boy said cheerfully, doffing his red cap to reveal short ginger hair. "I'm George."

"And I'm Sugar Martin."

His eyes widened. "From America?"

"You bet!"

"Do you know John Wayne?"

I stifled a giggle. "Nope. I've never met him." Seeing as how Hollywood wasn't exactly next door to Oregon.

Although crestfallen at my lack of silver screen connections, he nonetheless did his duty by me and my luggage, ushering us both inside. The lobby was small and carpeted in a wild, floral pattern of burgundy, pink, and gold which made me a little dizzy if I stared at it too long. George led me straight to the mahogany registration desk where a balding man with a bulbous nose peered over his gold-rimmed spectacles at me.

"Mr. Dix, this is Miss Martin," George said cheerfully. "She's come from America to stay with us."

"Indeed," said Mr. Dix who wasn't impressed in the least, if his snooty tone was anything to go by. "Welcome, Miss Martin. Have you a reservation?"

"Yes, it was made for me by my aunt's solicitor, Mr. James Woodward." Suddenly I was nervous. What if something had gone wrong and somebody had forgot to book the hotel for me? Or perhaps they hadn't paid for it? Wouldn't that be wacked out.

Mr. Dix riffled through a rectangular metal box. "Ahh... yes, here it is." He pulled out an index card. "You'll be staying with us for a week, is that correct?"

"Yes, I think so. I guess it depends on how long it takes to settle my aunt's will."

Mr. Dix looked bored. He pointed at the open registration book and the fountain pen next to it. "Sign here."

I did as instructed while he turned around and perused a selection of cubby holes. Some held mail or messages. Others were empty. And a few had shiny tags dangling from them. At last he selected one of the tags and withdrew a brass skeleton key which he handed to George.

"Here you are. Room six on the first floor." He pointed up, which confused me.

I'd no time to question him about it as he'd turned away. George was already ushering me toward elaborate Art Deco doors, my suitcases tucked under his arms.

"Isn't this the first floor?" I asked, as he stopped in front of the doors.

"No, Miss. We have to take the lift up. This is the ground floor. Isn't that what it's called where you're from?"

"We call it the first floor. And I guess what you call the first floor is what we refer to as the second."

"How dashed odd!" His eyes were wide, and he was obviously thrilled to be learning about our strange American ways.

"I guess it is." I laughed as the doors to the elevator—lift—swooshed open and we stepped inside. "Ground floor. It makes sense, I suppose." I eyed him, wondering if he'd been here during the war. Maybe he'd seen Sam. "Did you serve?"

"Serve what, Miss? Oh, you mean as a soldier. No, Miss. Too young. I was only fourteen when it ended. Spent the whole thing out near Bath with my auntie. Mum said London was too dangerous."

"She was probably right." I was strangely relieved that this bright, cheerful boy hadn't had to face the horrors of war. Perhaps it was silly of me, but if I could have waved a magic wand and created peace on Earth, I'd have done it. And Sam would still be with me—

I shoved that thought aside immediately. Sam was never coming back, and while I missed him, his voice had faded from my mind and even his image had grown hazy. All I had was a photograph and memories, and you can't build a life on that now, can you.

Onward! As Mama would say. Life is for the living, and I planned to live mine to the fullest.

My room proved to be quite small with a single bed and a narrow window overlooking a grim and gloomy alley. It was, however, clean, neat, and comfortable. The bathroom was at the end of the hall, and I had to share it with everyone else on the floor, which I found a little strange. Admittedly I hadn't stayed in many hotels, but I once stayed in a motel at the

Oregon Coast, and each of the rooms had their own bathrooms.

Ah, well. When in London!

I gave George a tip, and he went on his merry way.

I sat down on the bed to review the documents Mr. Woodward had sent me. Along with my ticket and hotel instructions was an itinerary for my first day. Since I would be arriving near luncheon, it was recommended that I dine at a cafe two blocks from my hotel. At precisely two in the afternoon, a car would arrive at the hotel to collect and deliver me to the offices of Woodward and Woodward, Solicitors. There I would meet with Mr. Woodward to discover at last the terms of my aunt's will.

I realized that my stomach was rumbling with hunger so, after a quick freshen up, I left my bags to unpack later and set out for the cafe. It was a little nerve wracking being alone in a strange country, but after a few fits and starts—the cars were all facing the wrong way, which I found confusing—I finally managed to get myself headed in the right direction. The café was on the ground floor of an Edwardian-era brick building that had escaped the ravages of the Blitz. There was a long counter behind which hung a blackboard marked with the daily specials. A number of small Formica-topped tables were scattered about, each with two uncomfortably rickety chairs. It wasn't exactly bright and cheerful, and I worried the food would match.

I found a seat near the window and ordered a bacon and cheese sandwich. I admit to being stunned at what I got. The bacon was more a fat-edged ham than anything resembling bacon, but the cheese was both sharp and nutty and the bread was homemade and delicious. Despite being ravenous, I only managed to eat half.

Returning to the hotel with my leftover sandwich and a bag of potato chips (The young woman behind the counter had called them crisps.) hidden in my handbag, I had plenty of time to unpack and hang my clothes in the wardrobe. Hopefully the wrinkles would come out, but for now they were not suitable for going out. My green suit would have to do, even if it was a bit travel worn and I was in dire need of a bath. I made do with a quick sponge-off and a spritz of Vent Vert perfume. I was sure the solicitor would understand.

When I reached the lobby, it was empty. No one behind the desk. No George hovering by the door. Suddenly I felt a tiny flutter of trepidation. I realized like never before that I was in a foreign city, an immense one compared to what I was used to, and I didn't know a soul. Unless you counted Mr. Woodward whom I'd never met. I didn't even know what he looked like!

I turned to glance at the clock perched above the elevator. The car was two minutes late. My nervousness only increased. What if they'd forgotten me?

"Buck up, Sugar," I muttered to myself.

"Pardon?"

The deep, masculine voice from behind startled me so badly I dropped my purse. The contents spilled across the carpeted floor, my lipstick—a lovely shade of matte red in a luxurious gold tube bought just for this trip—skittered beneath a chair. Both my compact and coin purse popped open, the now crumbled powder spilling onto the carpet along with an array of coins. I could have wept. Now I'd have to replace the powder, and I could ill afford to do so. I didn't turn around to chastise the newcomer, though you better believe I wanted to! Instead, I knelt and quickly gathered my things.

"So sorry." The voice was startlingly close to my ear this time.

I glanced over to find a man kneeling next to me. He wore a tidy navy-blue suit with a blindingly white shirt and a navy tie with a neat little gold and sapphire pin. Simple, but expensive. He was handsome in a bland way, with pale blond hair neatly slicked back into a small wave. The style was about five years out of date, but still perfectly acceptable and certainly attractive on him. His eyes were a grayish blue, his nose a little over large but perfectly straight, lips wide but thin, chin and jaw strong. And he smelled divine. I had no idea what cologne he was wearing, but it was no doubt expensive. I felt a strange, unexpected little flutter somewhere beneath my breastbone—something I hadn't felt since Sam—and repressed it ruthlessly. I wasn't here for romance. Not that he'd indicated in any way he was interested. I was being ridiculous.

"Here." He held out my lipstick which he'd fished from under the chair.

"Thank you," I said, suddenly overwhelmed with embarrassment. I shoved my other items back into my purse and stood so quickly we nearly locked bumpers. I hadn't realized he'd also risen. "Sorry. I seem to be a bit clumsy today." Were my cheeks really on fire, or did they just feel that way?

"No worries." He didn't smile or even look sympathetic. His face was an expressionless, almost arrogant mask. "May I assume you are Miss Euphegenia Martin?"

My spine stiffened. "You may not assume any such thing! However, you may tell me who *you* are." The nerve of this strange man.

He cleared his throat. "John Chambers. I was sent by Woodward and Woodward to collect Miss Martin."

"Oh." It sounded lame even to my own ears. "You're late." I almost winced at my rudeness, but discomfort in social situations often makes me blurt out things I probably shouldn't.

It seemed as if his cheeks darkened a bit, and his jaw may have clenched, but it was hard to tell. "My apologies, Miss Martin. You *are* Miss Martin." It wasn't a question.

"Yes. Yes I am."

"If you will accompany me. I've a car outside."

"Alright then." I lifted my nose ever so slightly in the air as I'd seen actresses do in the movies when they were trying to show a man he meant very little in the grand scheme of things. I wasn't entirely sure I pulled it off. Especially when I stumbled to a halt in the middle of the sidewalk.

"Is something wrong, Miss Martin?" Mr. Chambers asked as he held open the car door for me.

"Ah, no. Not at all." I eyed what I was absolutely positive was a Bentley, based on the little symbol stuck on the hood. I could hardly believe they'd sent such a fancy car for little old me. Sugar Martin of Portland, Oregon in a Bentley! The only time I'd ever seen a Bentley had been on a shopping trip downtown with Mama when Frederick Leadbetter drove by in his. Let me tell you, that was something I'd never forget.

I tried to behave as if I rode around in fancy cars all the time, but I think my wide-eyed stares and startled exclamations as we rode through the streets of London in style didn't fool anyone.

As the car swept along with a mighty purr of its engine, rain spat lightly against the windowpanes. The sky had gone from gloomy gray to downright grimly black. Still, I didn't let it deter me from enjoying the sights of elegant buildings standing like soldiers along the streets and the flash of green from little parks tucked away in back corners. And those little red calling boxes! I wanted desperately to make a phone call just so I could say I'd been in one.

At last we entered a section of town called Belgravia. I knew that not because Mr. Chambers told me—he'd been silent the entire ride, although he would occasionally cast a glance my way—but because I could see it on the plaques attached to each corner building. A few moments later, the driver stopped in front of an imposing white stone building very similar to my hotel, but quite a bit larger. And instead of a glass front door, it was solid wood painted red with a brass doorknocker in the shape of a lion.

Next to the door was a brass plaque engraved with the name Woodward and Woodward Solicitors, Est. 1705.

1705? Good heavens! They'd been around for ages.

Mr. Chambers showed me inside a rather impressive lobby. Certainly much more hoity-toity than my hotel lobby. The floors here were marble. The front desk was manned by a young gentleman in a brown suit with dark hair neatly pomaded into much higher waves than those Mr. Chambers sported. A crystal vase overflowing with tulips sat on the corner of the desk. Against one wall were a pair of leather club chairs and a low coffee table sitting on a blue Aubusson carpet, and the walls were hung with heavy oil paints of the English countryside.

"Is he in?" Mr. Chambers asked the young man without preamble.

"Yes, sir. Go on up."

"This way." Mr. Chambers indicated the staircase which wound upward around the oval wall.

As we ascended, I glanced up. The staircase continued up for four or five floors, leaving a sort of central atrium. Right above it was an oval skylight which let in watery gray light from above. I imagined on a sunny day it was quite lovely. Although it could use a few plants around to liven the place up.

We took the stairs all the way to the first floor, where Chambers rapped upon an unmarked door.

"Come." The voice was deep and masculine like that of Mr. Chambers, but it was also older and a bit hoarser, as if the owner had smoked a great deal.

Mr. Chambers opened the door and ushered me in first. A man sat behind a massive oak desk backlit by a window that took up nearly the whole back wall and overlooked a park. The trees outside where blindingly green with fresh, young leaves, or bright white with blossoms. Spots of color dotted the lush green lawn where flower beds had been planted.

After I'd been shown a seat and Mr. Chambers had been sent to obtain tea, I took a moment and let my eyes adjust. Mr. Woodward was more or less as I'd pictured him. Fit, handsome for an older gentleman, with a shock of white hair, dressed in a tailored black suit. He was precisely the sort of sophisticated person one expected in a lawyer. Or, in this case, solicitor. I wasn't entirely clear on the difference.

"Welcome to England, Miss Martin. I trust you had a pleasant journey?"

"Yes, thank you," I said, feeling instantly at ease in his presence.

"And you've settled into your hotel?"

"Oh, yes. It's very comfortable, thank you."

"Right, then I suppose we should get down to business." He picked up a pair of reading glasses and perched them on the end of his long nose.

I nodded. "That would be nice, yes." Nerves had crept in now, and I felt suddenly hot and prickly.

Before Mr. Woodward could say anything further, Mr. Chambers returned with tea. Once he'd poured us cups, Mr. Woodward said, "Would you please go and get Miss Martin's inheritance?"

Mr. Chambers nodded and once again exited the room.

"It's here?" I asked. "I expected to have to go to the bank or something." Or perhaps he was going to get a key. I'd inherited a house! Or a car! What would I do with a car?

"Your aunt was an unusual woman, Miss Martin," Mr. Woodward said. "She had no children of her own and no other relatives save those in America, the descendants of her sister. She chose you because you bore her name."

Which I'd more or less figured out on my own. What other reason would there be? "It's very kind of her."

"Indeed. And rather risky. So she made certain stipulations. It's complicated you see—"

The door once again opened, and Mr. Chambers reentered holding a leash on the end of which was... a dog. A short, fat, fluffy dog with perky ears and a long tail.

I stared at it. It stared at me with one blue eye and one gray, pink tongue lolling from its mouth.

"What is *that*?" I blurted.

Mr. Woodward almost seemed to squirm. "That, Miss Martin, is your inheritance."

Shéa MacLeod

Chapter 3

"Excuse me?"

I stared down at the mutt. It stared back at me, tongue lolling, gaze baleful. There was something inherently discomfiting in its mismatched gaze.

I cleared my throat. "I thought I heard you say this... animal... is my inheritance."

"That is correct." Mr. Woodward said, albeit a little uncomfortably. He shuffled some papers on his desk. "Miss Graves has left you her dog, Tippy. He's a Welsh Cardigan corgi."

What on earth? Dreams of a city apartment or a pile of cash went up in smoke. I straightened my spine. "I think you'd better explain."

Mr. Chambers handed me the leash, which I took reluctantly. I swear a smile twitched his lips. Mr. Chambers' lips, not the dog's. It wasn't that I disliked dogs. I liked them well enough, but *other* people's dogs. I'd never had any desire for one of my own. They always seemed so... unhygienic.

"Miss Graves was inordinately fond of animals," Mr. Woodward continued. "She was never without canine companionship throughout her long life—she was ninety-eight when she died. Despite her love of dogs, she had decided not to get another after her last one, Reginald, passed."

Reginald? Who named a dog Reginald?

"However, she fell in love with Tippy the moment she saw him. She decided that since she would likely outlive Tippy, she needed to make arrangements for him after her passing." He rustled the papers. "Hence her unusual will."

"Which I am still waiting for you to read," I said tartly.

Tippy whined and licked his lips. I guess he was getting impatient. Well, that made two of us.

"Very well, Miss Martin, the terms are fairly simple. Meeting them... that might be more difficult."

Wonderful. "Go on, Mr. Woodward."

"Miss Graves, while not wealthy, was comfortably off. She had a nice savings and a cottage in Devon, all of which she left to Tippy."

I blinked. "She left her estate to a dog? Is that even legal?"

"It is, I'm afraid. To you she left the conservatorship of Tippy for the term of his natural life. During which you will receive a small monthly stipend to pay for his keep and the upkeep and taxes on the house. When he passes, you will receive whatever is left of the money, as well as the cottage. Should Tippy die of other than natural causes, or if you fail to give him the proper care, you will forfeit both the money and the property." He laid the papers on the desk. "Any questions?"

So many. "I have to take care of this dog for the next ten or twenty years and then I'll get, what? A few hundred dollars and some rundown property? No thanks." I rose, intent on storming out. Although I'd no idea where I'd go. The plane ticket had been one way. I'd assumed because it might take some time for whatever legal processes were required, and I'd have the money to buy a return ticket when I was ready.

"It's more than a few hundred dollars." Mr. Woodward interrupted my intended exit. He mentioned a sum that nearly made me swallow my tongue. "And the cottage, while small, is quite lovely with a view of the sea."

A view of the sea? I'd always wanted a view of the sea. I cursed myself for being weak as I sank back down in my seat. "It'll be difficult to get a dog through customs."

"Oh, you can't take him back to America. The will stipulates that he is to stay here, in England, in his home. You must live in the cottage in Devon."

"B-but I can't stay here," I said, genuinely shocked.

"Why not?" Mr. Woodward asked. "You don't have a job, do you?"

"Well, no," I admitted.

"Then I don't see the problem. Mr. Chambers here," he waved to the younger man, "is tasked with checking up on you and Tippy periodically to ensure all is going well."

"To spy on me, you mean," I said dryly.

Mr. Woodward gave me a pained smile. "As you like."

"But I have family back home," I protested. Surely he saw that my staying in England was impossible.

"You will be allowed short visits home, and of course they can visit you here." As if that wasn't incredibly expensive.

Still, the idea of living in England, for a while at least, was tempting. Hadn't I always wanted an adventure?

I sighed. "Surely there must be some legal process to stay here."

"That's taken care of," Mr. Woodward assured me. "We will have your visa well in hand before your train leaves for Devon."

Oh, boy. "And when is that?"

"End of the week," he said. "It's already covered, so you needn't worry."

"And what about money? You said there was a monthly stipend."

He looked a little embarrassed. "Yes, for Tippy and the house. It will cover the necessaries such as food for Tippy, property taxes, electrical, water, all the basics. It will not cover food for yourself or any other of life's necessities."

I stared at him, jaw dropped. "So this... woman drags me over here, foists her dog on me, and then expects me to do what exactly?"

"Get a job," Mr. Chambers said dryly.

That got me steamed. "Are you insinuating I'm lazy?"

Mr. Woodward shot him a look. "I'm given to understand you were having difficulty finding a job in the States."

"I'm not sure how that is any business of yours, or how you knew about it, but yes, I was," I admitted. "If I were to stay in London, perhaps I could find something, but Devon? Is there a need for secretaries out there?"

"Is that your chosen career?" Mr. Woodward asked.

I frowned. "It's the only one available to women now that the war is over. Although I admit I'm not very good at it."

"Is that what happened at your last position?" Mr. Woodward asked.

"Ah, no. I was fired, but not for being bad at my job."

He lifted a brow.

"One of the male employees pinched my bottom one day. I slugged him in the kisser. I got fired." I shrugged. It was an unfortunate fact of life that women were harassed at their workplaces every day. We were just supposed to accept it. Unfortunately, I wasn't the accepting kind.

"And what did you do during the war?" he asked. "Perhaps you could do that."

"Welder. At the shipyards. We built warships, and I was good at it," I said proudly. "But they don't want women welders anymore."

"A pity," Mr. Woodward said, "however I believe I am in need of your services."

"Me?" I stared at him in astonishment. "But surely you know I'm a terrible secretary and besides, I can't stay here in London. You said so yourself. I have to live in Devon." I shot Tippy a dirty look. He promptly shot me one back. "Besides, you'd be much better off with someone else." Even if I really did need the job.

He gave me a long look. "One day, remind me to tell you about a marvelous, madcap woman I once met not long after the Great War. Maybe then you'll understand why I've no doubt you're up to the task. You see, I don't need your services as a secretary. I need your services as a spy."

"This is ludicrous," I said, posing in front of the gold-framed mirror and feeling absolutely ridiculous about it. Why had I agreed to this? Oh, yes, I needed a job.

"I think it looks rather nice," Mr. Chambers said, eyeballing my figure in a neat blue-and-white polka dot dress that fit snugly in the bosom before flaring out into a swirly skirt.

I shot him a glare. "I'm not talking about the dress, Mr. Chambers."

"I told you to call me Jack, Euphegenia."

"Only if you stop using that horrid name and call me Sugar."

"And you think Euphegenia is ridiculous," he muttered.

"What's that?" I arched a brow, hands on hips.

"Nothing." He stretched his legs and turned to the salesgirl. "We'll take that one. The red evening dress and the other day dresses. Do you have a trench? Perhaps something in pink."

"Jack," I snapped, "don't you agree this entire plan is ludicrous?"

"And yet you agreed to it."

"I didn't exactly have a choice." I marched into the dressing room to divest myself of the polka dot dress.

"You always have a choice," Jack called after me.

I ignored him. Perhaps he was right, but what choice *did* I have? It was either become a spy for Mr. Woodward's little investigation or ask my parents to wire enough money so I could go home. Not an appealing prospect. And so I chose the former.

It seemed Mr. Woodward had several wealthy clients with manor houses scattered around the country. Over the course of the last few months, many of them had thrown house parties during which they and their guests had been burgled, the thief making off with a fortune in valuables. After studying the pattern of thefts, he had come to the conclusion that the next place to be hit was a house party in Devon—in the very same village where my cottage was located—at the home of his friend and client, Lord Chasterly. He was convinced if he could get someone into the party undercover, that he or she could discover something of interest that might help him solve the case.

"Why don't you just call the police?" I'd asked.

"We have, of course. But the locals are useless, and this is the sort of thing one doesn't want bandied about."

"Well, then, why don't *you* go?" It seemed like a perfect solution. He was, after all, the one who'd been asked to investigate.

"I am well known in those circles. I don't want to risk the thief not showing up."

He'd had a point. I'd mulled it over. "What about Mr. Chambers? He is, after all, your employee."

"And my nephew. He is known as well."

I hadn't realized the two were related, though perhaps I should have with those strong jawlines and aristocratic noses. Not to mention the gray-blue eyes.

"Oh, very well," I'd agreed, knowing I needed the money. And surely being an undercover detective would be better than being a secretary. "But you're footing the bill."

"Of course. Shouldn't cost much."

I snorted. "That's what you think. You do realize that I don't have the wardrobe of an American heiress. I'll be found out immediately."

Which was how I'd ended up at a chic little boutique the very next day, trying on clothes with Mr. Chambers nearby in charge of the purse strings and to approve purchases. It felt oddly intimate to be shopping for clothes with a man. And one who was practically a stranger at that. Even more odd was shopping with a dog. But Tippy took it in stride and lay down under the divan for a nap.

The hotel people hadn't even blinked when I brought Tippy back with me. In fact, George had kindly scrounged up some scraps for the dog's dinner and taken him for a walk this morning.

"What do you know about this burglary business?" I asked Mr. Chambers—Jack—once he'd purchased a suitable number of outfits right down to the accessories.

I'd drawn the line at undergarments. For one thing, no one would see them, for another I couldn't fathom allowing a man to buy me lingerie. My mother would have a fit if she knew.

Mr. Woodward had suggested a lady's maid. I was supposed to be an heiress after all, but I'd said no. It would make more sense to stick closer to the truth. That I'd grown up without money and only come into it recently. That would cover up any faux pas a true heiress would never make. And such a woman would never bother with a maid. Mr. Woodward had, surprisingly, agreed with me. Probably because he could already see dollar signs swimming down the drain thanks to my new wardrobe.

"I only know what my uncle told you," Jack said, holding the door for me. "A number of his clients have been burgled recently. Always when in residence at their country homes, and always during a house party."

"Anyone other than your uncle's clients get robbed?" I asked.

"I'm not sure," he admitted. "It's been largely kept out of the papers. Why?"

"Because if it's only his clients being burgled, then that's an interesting clue. If others have been, it's merely a coincidence."

"Perhaps that's something you can ask once you get there."

I eyed him. "Perhaps." What I wanted to say was, "Obviously." But I bit my tongue. "How about this Lord Somebody I'm going to stay with?"

"Lord Chastlery was at school with Uncle Jamie. They've known each other for years. They cooked up this scheme together."

I lifted a brow. "This scheme?"

"Yes, the house party, the guest list... everything. Even you."

That was a surprise. "That's impossible. How could they have planned for my attendance? Surely the party was planned well in advance."

Jack inclined his head. "True. But they were looking for someone to fit the bill. If it wasn't you then it would have been someone else."

"Well, that's flattering," I said dryly.

"Don't take offense. Uncle has interviewed and rejected at least a dozen girls. He picked you almost instantly."

"Because I was desperate, I suppose."

"No, because he took a liking to you." He eyed me. "He doesn't take a liking to people easily."

"I sense that. Fine. I'm off to Devon to play heiress at a house party. I wish you could tell me more about the other burglaries. Or even who's attending this party. I won't know a soul."

"Maybe it's better you don't," he offered. "In that way, you will have a better chance at an honest first impression. You'll be seeing these people through fresh eyes instead of those colored by years of acquaintance or friendship."

"In other words, I'm less likely to be blind to their faults."

I swear he smirked. "Er, yes. Rather."

As we exited the shop, I made a beeline for the pharmacy down the street.

"Where are you going?" he demanded. "We've done our shopping."

"That's what you think. You owe me a new compact and some face powder. Now, who am I to report to?"

"Me. I'll be arriving in Devon the day after you do. My room is already booked at the local pub. I'll avoid the house as I could be recognized. When you have something to report, you can visit me in town, and we'll discuss your findings."

"And let me guess," I said. "You'll be checking up on this guy."

Tippy rolled his eyes up at me as if somehow knowing I was talking about him.

"Yes, I will. It's my job, after all."

How annoying. I felt like I was being babysat. Still, there wasn't a thing I could do about it, so I might as well get used to it. Besides, there are worse things that having a handsome man around. Even if his only interest was in my dog.

Chapter 4

"Well, Tippy, this may be the strangest adventure I have ever been on." I stared down at the mutt who lay panting at my feet. I'd been sure they wouldn't let him on the train, but Mr. Woodward had smoothed the way, much like he did everything else.

I still couldn't believe I was headed into the wilds of Devon with a stranger's dog and a key to a house that wasn't mine. Even stranger was the fact that, according to anyone who asked, I was an eccentric American heiress headed to a house party at Lord somebody or other's with the intent to spy for my new employer, Mr. James Woodward.

Strangest of all, perhaps, was that I now had a trunk filled with lovely clothes befitting such an heiress and more money to my name than I'd ever had at any one time, even when I was working as a welder. Mr. Woodward had opened an account for me and deposited my first paycheck as well as given me a small amount of cash as "walking around money."

The countryside flew by the window... green rolling hills dotted with fluffy white spots which could only be lambs, trees laden with fresh blossoms, and little thatched cottages so cute they made your teeth hurt. Eventually the greenery on one side gave way to an amazing view of the sea, almost painfully blue under the surprisingly sunny sky. It had been pouring down rain when I left London.

"You know, Tippy, this might not turn out so bad after all. Look at that view!"

Tippy heaved a grunting sigh as if he'd seen it all before. Maybe he had. Aunt Eupheginia's house was, after all, in Devon. He may well have taken this train before. Although based on his short legs, I doubt he'd seen much.

My stomach rumbled, and I pulled a cheese sandwich which I'd purchased at the station from my purse and unwrapped the waxed paper. I could have bought food on the train, but it seemed a waste of money. I wasn't even sitting in First Class. I was clear back in Third. I'd worried someone would notice, but Mr. Woodward assured me that the chauffeur who was to take me to the Endmere, Lord Whatsisname's manor, would meet me outside the station so he wouldn't notice which car I got out of. Mr. Woodward may have sprung for a new wardrobe, but he wasn't about to waste money on a First-Class ticket. In that, I suppose, we were of one mind.

I had, however, circumnavigated his plans somewhat. I'd caught an earlier train which would put me into the village of Meres Reach two hours before the chauffeur was meant to collect me at the station. I figured that would give me time to check out my new digs and drop off a few things I didn't necessarily want the other guests to see. Like my woefully inadequate American wardrobe.

I munched happily on my sandwich. It was quite a bit different than the cheese sandwiches I was used to back home. Mama frequently made them for lunches when I was a child since they were cheap and easy. Butter the bread, slap on cheese, done. If one was feeling fancy, one might fry them up on the stovetop.

The British cheese sandwich was a different kind of animal. Yes, there was bread and yes, there was cheese, but that was where the similarities ended. The woman at the sandwich counter had claimed the cheese was Cheddar, but it was sharper and more buttery than any Cheddar I'd ever tasted. Not to mention it was white instead of orange. In addition, there was a spread that looked a little bit like relish, except that it was brown and had a sweet, tangy, spicy flavor that went surprisingly well with the cheese.

Tippy lifted his head and snuffled excitedly, so I fed him a bit. He wolfed it down happily and snuffled again.

"Enough for you, mister. I'll let you have my crusts. I've never liked them much, though Mama always made me eat them. Waste not, want not." I chuckled as a memory came to me. "She also said all the good stuff was in the crust. Isn't that silly? It's all the same ingredients regardless of where in the loaf it is. It's not like it's an apple."

Tippy made a sort of muttering sound which I took to mean he agreed with me. As well he should. Maybe we would get along after all.

"I forgot to ask Mr. Woodward if Lord Something-or-other would mind me bringing you. I hope it's okay. I would hate to get off on the wrong foot," I mused.

Tippy whined as if he were also worried.

"You're cute, though, so that's in your favor."

There was a grunt of agreement. I guess he didn't have a problem with confidence.

Sandwich finished, I wadded up the wax paper and stuffed it back into my purse to be thrown out later. Then I retrieved a nub of a pencil and a small notebook which I always kept with me. I'm not sure why, but it seemed like a thing one should do, just in case one had a sudden bout of inspiration. Or needed to add to the shopping list.

"Let's see." I tapped on my lower lip with the pencil. "What's our first order of business when we get to the manor?"

Tippy rolled his eyes toward me, then away. He let out a deep, huffing sigh and rested his chin on his outstretched paws.

"Well, you're no help. Let me think... I'll speak to Lord Whoever-he-is. That's the most important thing, right? He is, after all, the one who hired us." I jotted that down.

Tippy ignored me.

"Next, I need to find out which other houses were robbed and if all the owners were clients of Mr. Woodward or not."

I wrote that under the heading of "no. 2."

"I should also try and get guest lists from the other house parties. That way I can compare which guests were at which parties. I'm betting it *is* a guest. Or maybe a servant. How else would they get away without anyone noticing? It's obvious, don't you think?"

Another eye roll from Tippy. So far, he was proving useless as an investigative partner.

At last the train rolled into the Meres Reach Railway Station.

"Come along, Tippy," I said.

Tippy trotted dutifully behind as I exited the train along with a small crowd of Londoners clearly on vacation with their casual clothes and suitcases. My own suitcases were soon piled on a trolley manned by an ancient denizen who looked like a stiff breeze could blow him over.

"Moving to Meres Reach?" he asked.

"Yes." Tippy barked and I remembered I was under cover. "I mean no. I mean... temporarily. I've been invited to a house party."

"Lot of that going around."

I wasn't sure what he meant and didn't have time to ask. "Is there a place I can get a taxi?"

"Sure, Miss. Right out front. Ain't nothing fancy like London Town, but Old Tom does his best."

I wondered how old Old Tom must be for this wizened man to refer to him that way. Which was why I was stunned to find him a young-ish man of forty-something but with a very old, very bright green truck. After seating me and Tippy up front where we both tried to dodge exposed seat springs, he tossed my luggage—including one body-sized trunk—into the bed like they weighed no more than feathers. Then he jumped into the driver's seat.

"Where to, Miss?" Little crinkles fanned out from his eyes. Now here was a man who enjoyed a good laugh.

"Number two, Sea Breeze Lane," I said, peering at the cramped hand-written instructions I'd been given. Jack had terrible writing.

Old Tom's eyes widened in surprise. "Miss Grant's cottage?"

Well, shoot. No use now in trying to hide anything. Hopefully, none of the people attending the party would have any reason to ask around about my living situation.

"Yes. I'm her niece, you see—"

"Say no more." He revved the engine. "Thought I recognized the little mutt there. Welcome back, Tippy."

Tippy woofed.

"And welcome to Meres Reach, Miss...?"

"Martin. Sugar Martin. Don't ask."

He grinned. "Wasn't going to. Sugar sounds sweet to me." And with a boisterous laugh, he pulled out of the parking lot and into the almost non-existent traffic.

The train station sat on a flat bit of land which nudged up against a tangled forest. Above it rose an imposing cape which jutted out onto the water. Perched at the very end was a building which glittered under the watery sun. Below the station, the ground sloped away gently down toward the sea. A ribbon of road ran down the slope all the way to the water, and on either side huddled gorgeous little stone cottages with colorful doors and window boxes overflowing with flowers. Almost as if they were posing for a post card.

About halfway down this main street, Old Tom turned right onto Ocean View Road and then took a right onto Sea Breeze Lane. Two doors down was an itty, bitty stone cottage with a thatched roof and wisteria arching above the door. The door and shutters, now closed, were painted a pale lavender. Tippy sat up and sniffed the air happily as if he knew he was almost home.

As for a sea view, I guess you could say there was one. If you stood on tiptoes on the front stoop and craned your neck.

"Here you are, Miss. You want I should bring in your luggage?"

"Yes, please. Everything but the blue suitcase and the train case."

He glanced into the bed of the truck. "What do you want me to do with them then?"

How would he take this? "I'll need you to take me back to the station with them in..." I checked my wristwatch, "...twenty minutes."

He stared at me. "I gotta admit, Miss, that's a strange request."

"I'm going to a house party, you see. And the chauffeur is going to pick me up at the station." There, hopefully that didn't let the cat out of the bag completely.

"Oh, gotcha. It's that party up at the big house."

"You know about it?"

"Sure. Everyone does. Well, let's get you settled then." He hopped out, rounded the truck, and held the door for me like a proper gentleman.

While I dug out the key Mr. Woodward had given me, Old Tom wrestled my luggage out of the back of his truck. I pushed open the door to a wave of dried roses, dust, and dog. Tippy yipped and rushed straight in. I took a deep breath of fresh air before plunging in, leaving the door open for Old Tom.

There wasn't much to see. You walked straight into the living room, which was crammed with old furniture, heavy oil paintings, and enough crocheted doilies to choke a horse. There was an open doorway which led into a small kitchen just large enough for a sink, stove, and a table for two. Other than the table, there was no counter space. Everything either hung from wall hooks or sat on open shelves on the wall.

There were two doors in the kitchen. One, which Tippy sat in front of, led to a back yard so small you could hardly turn around in it. There were a couple of flowerpots filled with dead plants and a square of grass just large enough for Tippy to do his business. Which he proceeded to do.

Leaving him to it, I explored the second door. It led to a bedroom hardly big enough to fit a full-sized bed, and beyond that, the world's smallest bathroom. Although it was large enough to have a tub. Of sorts. It was more like a half tub. I could maybe sit down if I twisted myself into a pretzel.

So this is where I was going to live from now on. It wasn't terrible, though it was probably smaller than my apartment, which was an astonishing feat. A good airing was what it needed. Yes, I could do this. Sure I could.

"Where you want your chest, Miss?" Old Tom shouted from the front room.

Since there was nowhere to put anything in the bedroom—the miniscule cupboard was still full of Aunt Euphegenia's things—I had him leave everything sitting neatly behind the couch. I'd have to deal with it all later. Once I figured out if I could get rid of my aunt's ancient wardrobe, or if that, too, belonged to Tippy.

"Would you like a coffee or something before we go?" I asked Old Tom.

He glanced dubiously around the kitchen. "Wouldn't mind a cup of tea, Miss. If you've got it. Want me to show you how to turn on the cooker? Might be different where you come from."

"Thank you, but I think I can manage." The gas stove was surprisingly modern, white enamel with black fittings. I suddenly worried the gas had been shut off after my aunt's death, but a twist of the knob gave away to the tell-tale hiss of gas. I grabbed a box of matches off the shelf and had it lit in no time.

After enjoying a cup of tea, albeit without milk since the ridiculously small fridge had been emptied and turned off, we chugged back up the hill where Old Tom handed me off to the ancient porter, along with Tippy and my suit and train cases. As Tom drove off, the porter didn't even question my reappearance or the fact that I didn't want to board a train. We all scuttled back to the train platform.

Just in time as a man in a gray uniform appeared. "Miss Martin?"

"Yes. That's me."

"I am Marks, Lord Chasterly's driver. Your car is waiting."

Lord Chasterly. *That* was his name.

Mr. Woodward and I had agreed that I would use my real name. It was easier and, if anyone tried to look me up, they'd discover that I was indeed an American heiress. And since no one but Mr. Woodward and Mr. Chambers—and Old Tom and maybe the entire village of Meres Reach— knew the truth about my inheritance, my cover would hold.

I followed the chauffeur through a red brick arch. Tippy followed me, and the ancient porter followed Tippy with the trolley. I felt guilty about that. I was probably stronger than he was, but I had to maintain my image as a rich woman. That did not include pushing around trolleys and getting sweaty.

The car was even fancier than Mr. Woodward's Bentley. For one, it was a newer Bentley. Brand new as far as I could tell. It was a rich cream with a slightly darker cream roof and matching interior of buttery soft leather. There was even a well-stocked burlwood bar. Whoever heard of a bar in one's vehicle?

The chauffeur held open the door and didn't even blink when Tippy hopped in after me. I had a sudden nightmarish vision of the dog tearing up the upholstery, but my aunt must have trained him well, for he curled up on the floor and went immediately to sleep.

Being from Oregon, I am used to lush greenery, but the countryside that spread out around me was beyond verdant. Like something out of a painting. Tangles of forest hugged the sides of the narrow road. The story book village exploded in a riot of flowers huddled along the water's edge, while a church spire poked up against a brilliant blue sky. We trundled over a stone bridge beneath which tumbled a babbling brook. And in the distance the sea rolled endlessly toward shore.

The manor house was some distance above Meres Reach clinging to the cliff above the seaside village. The village itself sat mere inches from the water, little sherbet colored buildings marching up and down the promenade while colorful boats rocked in the bay.

We wound through the cobblestone streets, past a pub and a cafe and a greengrocer, until we came to a curlicued wrought-iron gate. Just on the other side of it, we passed a gatekeeper's cottage with a thatched roof—adorable!—and a garage with multiple bays, then zoomed up along the cliffside, hugging the rock wall, a sheer cliff on the other side.

At last we pulled up onto the rocky promontory and saw the house itself, a stark white Georgian manor with Greek columns and square windows that gleamed in the sun. Thick shrubs hugged the house, overflowing with colorful dark pink blossoms.

Marks hopped out and opened my door just as what could only be a butler appeared. Along with him was a tousled-haired boy of about fifteen—who looked like he belonged working in a garden—and a girl not much older in a maid's uniform. The two kids helped themselves to my luggage, while the butler offered me a scant bow.

"Welcome to Endmere, Miss Martin. I am Johnson. I hope your stay here is a pleasant one."

"Thank you, Mr. Johnson."

He looked pained. "Just Johnson, Miss. Follow me, please."

The foyer was as amazing as the exterior. The floor was set out in a diamond pattern with lighter and darker hardwoods. A crystal chandelier hung from an ornate medallion. To my left was a staircase carpeted in blue floral fabric, while straight ahead through a wide arch I could see a comfortably furnished living room.

"I am certain you will wish to wash up before you meet your host." It wasn't a question. In fact, it was just this side of an order. "Penny will show you your room."

A second maid popped out of thin air. She was older than the first one, but still at least ten years my junior, making her barely past eighteen. Her head of coppery red curls only half hidden by an old-fashioned mob cap matched her moniker.

"I will happily take your... dog." Johnson said the last word with disdain.

I would have loved for him to take Tippy off my hands, but instead I said, "That's alright. I'll keep him with me. Though he probably needs something to eat and some water."

Whatever Johnson thought of that, he kept wisely to himself. "Very well. I will have something brought to your rooms. Penny can take him out later."

"Sure I can," Penny said cheerfully. "If you'll follow me, Miss." She demurely led me up the stairs and down the hall to the third door on the right. "This is where you'll be staying, Miss. His lordship just had it redone. Has its own wash room and everything." She opened the door with a dramatic flourish.

I stepped inside and stopped with my mouth hanging open. Tippy did the same. Whether from shock or simply because he wanted to lie down, it was hard to tell. You could have fit Aunt Eephegenia's entire cottage in that one room.

The walls had been painted midnight blue and the carpet was a damask midnight blue and gold. On the wall above the bed was painted a rather gaudy mural of a basket of flowers which was mimicked on the matching midnight blue nightstands. In fact, all the furniture—from the vanity seat to the armchair and ottoman to the blinds on the windows—was midnight blue. All the soft furnishings were sheer, ruffled, and very pink. Pink curtains with ruffles trimmed in midnight blue ribbons, pink vanity cloth swathed in ruffles tied up with the same color ribbons. Even the bedspread bore pink ruffles and blue ribbons. There was even a pink robe and matching pink slippers laid out for my use.

"Isn't it lovely?" Penny cooed.

"It's... a lot of pink." I managed.

"I know! I just love pink! Can't wear it with my hair though." She looked crestfallen.

I decided it would be better not to comment on her hair color. "You said there was a bathroom?" I nudged.

"What? Oh, yes, this way." She opened a door to reveal more pink.

The floor was a midnight blue linoleum, the walls stark white tile, but the bathtub, sink, and toilet were all pink. Even the curtain around the tub was pink with those ridiculous blue ribbons. Good grief.

"Very nice," I managed.

It wasn't that I minded pink. It was just that there was an awfully lot of it.

There was a loud thump from the bedroom.

"That'll be Billy with the luggage," she said. "I'll get you unpacked, and you have a nice freshen up." Before I could answer, she'd exited, pulling the bathroom door shut behind her.

I stared at my reflection in the mirror. "Sugar Martin, what have you gotten yourself into?"

Tippy whined. I hoped that meant he was hungry and not that things were about to go terribly wrong.

By the time I'd finished washing up and exchanged my new lavender travel suit for a silk robe, Penny was done hanging my clothes in the wardrobe. She'd even managed to get one of my dresses pressed. A pretty teal dress with a bow at the neckline, shirred sleeves, and a light shirring to the skirt to give it the right amount of fullness. It was perfect for afternoon wear and even a semi-formal cocktail party, as Mr.

Woodward assured me would take place early every evening. I paired it with black duo-strapped shoes with peep toes and simple gold jewelry.

The jewelry wasn't terribly expensive, but it looked like it was. Mr. Woodward had assured me that it was excellent gold plate, completely indiscernible from solid gold. He was determined to ensure I was tempting to the burglar.

Penny showed me the way to the living room, not that I needed it, but I was grateful for her cheerful chatter. "You'll never believe who's coming." Her bright eyes shone. "Lady Antonia. She arrives tomorrow. I overheard Mrs. Mills—that's the housekeeper—telling Francois—that's his lordship's French chef. Apparently, he has a very discerning palate. Whatever that means." She giggled.

"Who is Lady Antonia?" I couldn't remember Mr. Woodward or Mr. Chambers mentioning her.

"She's the widow of the Earl of Netherford," Penny explained in a low voice as we descended the stairs. "Technically, she's the Countess of Netherford or Lady Netherford.

There's no new Lady Netherford, you see, since her husband died without an heir, so she wouldn't have to use the term Dowager, like most widows. But Lady Antonia insists on being terribly informal. It drives Johnson and Mrs. Mills absolutely batty!"

"Good grief, it's all so confusing," I said. "We don't have all these titles in America. It's just Miss, Mrs, or Mr. Well, unless you're a doctor or a professor or something."

"You should have a good time now Lady Antonia will be here," she confided. "She's sure to make things interesting. She always does. Well, here you are. Go on in and make yourself comfortable. I'll tell his lordship. And don't worry about Tippy. I'll take good care of him."

"Thank you, Penny."

The living room—or I suppose the British would probably call it a drawing room or something fancy like that—was a surprisingly feminine room. The walls were painted a pale blue with drapes in a floral pattern of the same color to match. To one side was a white marble fireplace in which a low fire burned, built-in bookshelves on either side were stuffed with books and curios from around the world. Above the mantle hung a series of paintings of various birds in shades of blues and yellows. On one side of the fireplace sat two chairs in yellow, blue, and pink floral with a simple antique table between them and opposite sat a comfortable looking sofa in a blue and white damask the same color as the drapes. In the middle of the seating arrangement was a low coffee table painted the same yellow as the chairs and on which sat a heavy glass ashtray and a selection of colorful magazines.

Maybe when I got home, I could decorate my place like this. Well, the cheap version. Then I remembered Devon was my home now. I wasn't sure how I felt about that.

Since I was alone in the room, I took a seat in one of the chairs as they faced the door and selected a magazine which featured the homes and lifestyles of Britain's rich and famous. I was deep into an article on Lady Somebody's fondness for peonies when the French doors behind me were flung open accompanied by a gust of chilly air from outside.

I started, whirling to face the newcomer. Dressed in what I could only assume was hunting gear based on the shotgun held in the crook of his arm, he was nearly as broad as he was tall, with a florid face and eyebrows in need of trimming. He was around the same age as Mr. Woodward, but while Mr. Woodward was calm and matter of fact, this man was loud and blustery.

"What, ho! Is that Miss Martin at last? Old Jamie said you were on your way. Come to assist us with our little problem, I hear." There was a bit of eyebrow waggling and suggestive winking, and I could only assume "Old Jamie" was a reference to Mr. Woodward as his given name was James.

"Yes, that's so, Lord—" Oh, dear what was his name? Oh, yes! "Lord Chasterly."

He let out a braying laugh just as Johnson appeared to take his hat, coat, and gun. Once divested of these items and with Johnson out of the room, he said, "Call me Freddy. Everyone does."

"Sure. Freddy. I'm Sugar."

His eyes widened. "That's an actual name? I though Jamie was having a laugh."

I grinned good-naturedly. "Unfortunately, my actual name is much worse. I prefer Sugar."

"Then Sugar it shall be. Drink?" He turned toward a cabinet on the other side of the room and began pulling out bottles of liquor.

"Um, sure."

"I know it's not summer yet, but I fancy a daiquiri."

"That sounds nice." I wasn't much of a drinker, but when I did imbibe, I enjoyed a good cocktail.

He dumped ice and an enormous amount of rum into a cocktail shaker, added from a bottle of some sort of yellowish-green juice, and then a clear liquid which I hoped was simple syrup and not more alcohol. He gave it all a vigorous shake and then filled two martini glasses to the brim. I was astonished he didn't spill a drop on the way to deliver it.

I took a sip and almost hacked up a lung.

He chuckled. "What can I say? I like 'em strong."

"I see that." I took another sip, more gingerly this time. It actually wasn't bad.

"Now," he said, settling back on the sofa and ignoring a clump of dirt which had dislodged itself from his boot and fallen on the carpet, "Jamie told you why you're here, correct?"

"Yes. He said there's been a string of burglaries at the country homes of his clients. They were all holding house parties at the time. He is of the opinion you may be next."

"Indeed. Because I planned it that way." He gave me a shrewd look that made me realize that perhaps his boisterous exterior was just that, a shell to hide a very keen intellect. "Here is what we know." He settled in and took a long drink. "There have been four houses hit so far. Mine will be the fifth."

I wondered how he could be so sure. "Are all of them Mr. Woodward's clients?"

"Three of the five."

So Mr. Woodward's office wasn't the key. "Go on."

"Each house was hit during a house party, as you know. The guests were the cream of British society. Very wealthy. Very connected. Every guest had something stolen... jewelry, cash—though not much of that—and in one case a very expensive mink stole."

"All things that can be easily sold, I assume."

He nodded approvingly. "Yes, indeed."

"Were the same people at every party?"

"Many of the same, yes. Though there were differences. I'm certain you can scrounge up a list from Mr. Woodward or one of his assistants."

"Yes," I agreed. "I'm to meet one of them tomorrow."

"Jolly good." He drained his glass and rose. "Another?"

"Not at the moment, thank you." I'd barely taken two sips.

He sauntered over and refilled his glass. Once he was seated again, I hit him with another question.

"What time of day did the burglaries take place?"

"All times. The first was at night. Everyone was asleep and the thief simply went from room to room liberating whatever he pleased. Dashed cheeky of him."

I didn't disagree. "And the others?"

He frowned and mulled it over. "The second was also at night, while the third was in the middle of the day."

"You're joking. Talk about cheek!"

"Indeed, young lady. He's a brazen one."

"How did no one see him? There must have been people everywhere."

"I wasn't at that particular event, but my understanding is that all the guests save the lady of the house were out attending an event in the village. The lady was down with a headache, and the maids had been banished below stairs so as not to disturb her. In he went, took what he liked, walked out bold as brass."

"And the fourth?" I asked.

"The fourth was during a masked ball. Mostly rifled through the guests' rooms which were empty, but it appears he may have lifted jewelry right off one guest."

"Good heavens!" The brazenness of the thief was astonishing. "I assume the police are involved."

"As much as we'll allow them to be. We don't want word getting out, so we haven't exactly let them have free reign."

Which was astonishing. I couldn't imagine telling the Portland Police Department they weren't allowed to investigate a case. They'd probably throw you in jail for withholding evidence or something.

"And you've no idea who the perpetrator might be?" I was proud of knowing the lingo. I'd seen enough Hollywood movies, after all. Not to mention all the detective novels I'd read. Maybe I could really do this.

"I'm afraid not. It's difficult to investigate without giving ourselves away, you see."

I nodded. "I get it. These are your peers. The people with whom you must deal on a regular basis both personally and in business. Ruffling feathers would no doubt be costly."

He grinned. "Jamie was right. You're one bright cookie."

"Thank you." I studied him a moment. "Lord Chasterly—Freddy—why are you willing to trust me? A stranger and a woman at that." It wasn't often that I found a man willing to entrust a woman with a shopping list, never mind a criminal investigation.

He gave me a long look over the rim of his glass. "If you're good enough for Jamie Woodward, you're good enough for me." He stood up, his old Bonhomme was back. "Another daiquiri?"

"Why not." Because apparently our meeting was over, and I was none the wiser.

Chapter 5

As it turned out, I was the first of the guests to arrive. All the rest were scheduled for the next day. His lordship clearly didn't view me as a true guest and sent his apologies for dinner via Penny. I wasn't about to sit alone in the massive formal dining room, so I took my dinner—or supper, as she called it—in my room.

It turned out to be a rather nice evening. I didn't have to get dressed up or try and pretend to be somebody I wasn't. Instead, I ate in my new silk pajamas—luxury! —while polishing off the Christie novel I'd brought with me.

I was determined to put the whole investigation out of my mind, but it was a difficult thing to do. I mean, who'd have ever thought it! Me, Sugar Martin, an undercover agent. It was so... Scarlet Pimpernel.

Mr. Chambers—Jack—would be arriving in Meres Reach late morning. I was to meet him for lunch at the pub, the Sullen Oyster. It seemed so scandalous, a woman in a pub, but Penny assured me that as long as I was accompanied, the Sullen Oyster was a perfectly acceptable place for a lady. Hopefully Jack would have more information for me.

I was also really keen to meet this Lady Antonia Penny rambled on about. She sounded fascinating.

I had managed to get a guest list from Penny, such as it was. She'd scrawled it on the notepad on my desk. Her handwriting was like chicken scratch and difficult to make out, but I managed.

Lady Antonia was, of course, first. The only thing Penny had written was "I already told you about her."

"Yes, Penny, very helpful," I murmured, licking the last of the peach crumble and custard off my spoon.

Simon and Mary Parlance were next. "Honourables," Penny had written. Whatever that was. "Twins. Supposed to be v. rich." I assumed the v stood for "very." Curious about the use of "supposed." Were they not so rich after all? Had they lost all their money, perhaps? That might put them in dire straits. Were they the ones behind the thefts? Or maybe Penny just didn't know what their status was. It was impossible to tell.

I had to squint at the next line. "Lady Fortescue. Single. Has it bad for… his lordship." Well, that was interesting. Freddy was handsome for an older man, so I could understand this Lady Fortescue having a crush on him, but what could her motive for theft be? Or did she even have one?

Next on the list was a Mr. Raymond somebody. It looked like the surname started with an F, but it was hard to tell it was so badly written and a bit smudged. All Penny had written about him was "don't know."

And finally, a Mr. Alexander Malburn. To which Penny had concluded, "I think he's an heir to a barony or something."

Including my host and myself, that meant there were four men and four women at this house party. It didn't seem like a large selection from which to steal, but if they were all supposedly wealthy, perhaps it would be tempting to the thief.

On the bottom of the page in more of Penny's sprawling hand was, "Party on Saturday, everyone invited. Not just houseguests."

I had no idea who "everyone" encompassed, but I was betting it meant lots more rich people which meant many more targets for the thief. It also meant the thief might not be one of the main guests at all, but someone from the greater pool of guests.

"You know," I said to Tippy who was snoring gently next to the bed, "this is proving a little more difficult than I thought it would be. How does Mr. Woodward think I could possibly figure this out?" Welding I could do. Secretarial work... well, that was a little iffier. But solving a crime? It was a good thing that, in addition to Christie, I read all those dime store detective novels. The ones women weren't supposed to read. As if that ever stopped me.

"Yes, I think I've fallen off the deep end. But desperate times call for desperate measures."

Tippy ignored me and I went back to reading the latest edition of Ellery Queen's Mystery Magazine. I must have dropped off at some point, for something startled me awake. Disoriented, I stared around the room trying to figure out where I was and why I wasn't asleep. The reading lamp was still on, and the clock read two in the morning.

Tippy stared up at me from his place on the floor, ears cocked. I didn't know much about dogs, but I had a feeling that meant something. What had roused the both of us?

I got up and padded barefoot to the bathroom to get myself a glass of water. The tile was chilly beneath my feet, and cold air whispered in through the window that had been left slightly cracked. It was then I heard a sort of tumbling sound followed by a crash and a mumbled curse word that shouldn't be repeated in public.

I froze. The room on the other side of the wall was reserved for the incoming guests. Penny had told me as much, though she hadn't been sure who was assigned to that room. Still, there shouldn't have been anyone there as the guests didn't arrive until tomorrow. Or rather, later today.

Creeping back into my room, I snapped at Tippy. "Come on, Tip. There's an intruder. Time to be fierce." I wasn't sure a corgi could be fierce, but I was willing to give it a shot if he was.

Tippy let out a soft groan rife with annoyance and heaved himself to his feet. I opened the door as quietly as I could, and together we padded out into the hallway and along the corridor to the next door. There were definite sounds of movement.

I glanced down and gave Tippy a nod. I swear he nodded back.

Bracing myself, I thrust the door open and shouted, "Got you!"

The woman on the other side let out a shriek and threw something which crashed against the doorframe and smashed into a thousand pieces. I barely managed to duck. Tippy let out a yelp. And then the three of us were facing off like something out of a gangster movie.

The dark-haired woman dressed in a frothy yellow peignoir pointed a letter opener at me. A sharp looking thing that had my heart beating faster. "Who the devil are you? And what are you doing in my room?"

"Your room?" I gasped.

Tippy yelped helpfully.

"Yes." She tilted her head back revealing a stunningly beautiful heart-shaped face off-set by a widow's peak and a single shock of white hair in the dark. She was about ten years older than me but with a beauty I could only dream about. "I am Lady Antonia, and this is *my* room. Now who the devil are you?"

I nearly wilted with relief, which was followed closely with embarrassment. "I'm Sugar Martin, one of the other guests. I'm sorry. I just—I heard a noise in here, and I thought... the other guests weren't supposed to arrive until tomorrow. Well, today now."

"Exactly. I arrived today just as I said I would." She grinned and tucked the letter opener away on the dainty white desk.

I breathed a sigh of relief. "Sorry. I just... I didn't realize. Um, welcome?" The last came out lame, but it was the best my befuddled brain could manage.

She laughed lightly. "No worries. It's the most exciting thing that's happened all day."

She winked. "And who's this little darling?" She knelt down and gave Tippy a rub under the chin which sent him into ecstasy.

"Tippy. He's my au—he's my dog."

Tippy turned his head and gave me a baleful look. Apparently he didn't consider himself my dog.

"Simply adorable. I do love dogs, but I travel so often it doesn't seem fair to keep one of my own, you know?" She rose.

"Oh, sure." I didn't bother to tell her that I wouldn't have this dog if he hadn't been thrust upon me. I doubted she would understand. Dog people never do. "I am sorry to bother you. I should go back to my room."

"Oh, no! Please stay. I rarely get the chance for girl talk. Have a seat. I've got something lovely stashed in my trunk." She grinned devilishly and dived into the steamer trunk that still sat in the corner. She came back up with a pair of crystal tumblers and a bottle of port.

Since it would be rude to refuse, I accepted a glass of ruby liquid as I sat cross-legged on her bed. Her room was a mirror image of mine with pink walls and accents instead of blue, and navy soft furnishings instead of pink.

Unlike me, Lady Antonia was just as frothy as her room and just as lovely. Despite being silly o'clock, her face was done up perfectly with ruby red lips, moonglow skin, and her eyes were done with a line of black eyeliner along the top lid and a single rich blue color blended in. I wasn't sure if her eyelashes were naturally that thick and dark or if she were using mascara. She was stunningly beautiful, and I could see why Penny got a bit giddy when talking about her.

"So, tell me about yourself," she said, draping herself elegantly on the bed, a glass of port dangling from one hand. "What sort of a name is Sugar?"

"A nickname," I explained. "My father gave it to me when I was young, and it sort of stuck."

"Well, if I'm to call you Sugar, you should call me Toni. All my friends do." She grinned and a dimple popped in her cheek.

I felt an unexpected rush of warmth that this glorious creature wanted me to be her friend. Perhaps that was silly, but I didn't have many friends. All mine had gotten married, had children, and no longer had time for a spinster. I so did hope Toni wasn't the thief.

"You're from America?" She took a sip of her wine.

"Yes. Oregon. On the West Coast."

"Never heard of it. Is it near Hollywood? I do adore Hollywood!"

I repressed a grin. "Close." If close meant more than a thousand miles. "Have you been to Hollywood, then?" I never had, though it sounded terribly exciting and glamorous.

"Oh, no," she said. "But it sounds marvelous doesn't it? All those gorgeous film stars."

I agreed wholeheartedly.

Over the next hour I discovered that Lady Antonia was, as Penny had claimed, a widow and a rather merry one at that. She and Lord Chasterly were old friends having more or less grown up together, although she was "quite a bit younger." Her words, not mine.

"He's always after me, you know," she confided. "Thinks he'd make an excellent second husband. Let me tell you, I've no intention of having any more husbands. Too much trouble. But he does throw the best parties."

"Do you go to a lot of house parties in the country?" I asked, thinking of all the various ones that had been burgled.

"As often as possible, but I've been in the South of France for the past few months, so I've missed out on quite a lot."

Which meant she probably wasn't the thief. I was oddly relieved, as I truly liked her.

After two or three glasses of port and a bit of gossip about people I'd never heard of, I managed to beg off and return to bed, Tippy at my side.

"Well, that was interesting," I said as I crawled back under the covers.

He agreed.

Meres Reach was entirely adorable close up. I hadn't gotten a good look when I'd viewed Aunt Euphegenia's cottage, but I was thrilled to see the sort of place I'd be living in. The cobbled streets, though difficult to walk on in heels, were beyond charming. The shops, huddled close together in their ice cream colors, begged me to enter. The sun overhead urged me to enjoy the sea breeze awhile longer. But I had business to attend to.

I'd woken surprisingly early after my morning tryst with Toni. Johnson had been startled to see me up and about, but had nonetheless provided me with eggs, toast, and coffee. He'd muttered an apology about not having a proper breakfast ready, but I assured him it was all I needed.

After breakfast, I'd informed him I was taking Tippy for a walk. Tippy was not at all pleased about the distance to town, but I didn't want anyone in the house knowing where I was going or why, so I didn't dare ask for a lift.

The Sullen Oyster sat facing the bay, its half-timbered beams dark with age and the hand painted sign showing what looked more like a clam than an oyster, though it was definitely cranky. I wondered where it had gotten its very strange name.

I felt a bit nervous about entering a pub. It didn't seem like a place a lady would go, but I reminded myself I was an *investigator* and made of sterner stuff. "You stay here, Tippy." I tied him to a post outside the door. I was betting it was made for hitching horses back in the day. "I won't be long." I hoped.

Tippy gave me a disgusted glare and settled down to wait.

Was that a stab of guilt I felt? Surely not!

The pub was dim and warm and smelled of yeast and tobacco with a haze of bluish smoke permanently settled in the air. The ceiling was low with heavy oak beams and a low fire burned in a stone fireplace, blackened with soot. All eyes turned toward me as I entered. No doubt because I was the only female in the place. I blushed furiously, but straightened my shoulders, tilted my chin, and marched in.

"Miss Martin, over here!"

Jack sat in a corner booth with a good view over the street to the bay. I hurried to join him, relief flooding me. At least I wasn't alone. All those stares made the skin between my shoulders twitch. Although, once I was with my escort, everyone else lost interest.

"Should you really shout my name out like that in public," I hissed as I approached the table.

"I wouldn't worry. Nobody from Endmere would be seen in this place, except maybe

Freddy and he knows who you are. Maybe we should go outside," he said as I slid into the booth. The rich wood of the table shone dully in the faint light streaming in from the window. "I don't think they're used to women here."

"What if someone sees us together?" I argued. "Our cover will be blown. They'll just have to deal with it." I set my chin stubbornly.

He grimaced. "Very well. How are you settling in?"

"Fine. Lord Chasterly and his staff are very kind. And I just met the first guest, Lady Antonia. She showed up in the middle of the night."

He raised a brow. "That's odd, isn't it?"

"Not for her, or so says Penny."

"Penny?"

"That's the maid. She tells me Toni is something of a free spirit. Lord Chasterly has a bit of a thing for her, but Toni isn't interested."

"She still showed up, though," he pointed out.

I nodded. "Yes, but I'm not sure that means anything. She enjoys parties and socializing, and I don't know yet who was at the other parties."

"Ah, as to that. I have a list." He pulled a folded piece of paper from the inner breast pocket of his suit coat and spread it flat on the table.

"Perfect! Just what I needed." I peered at the neatly typed sheet.

There were five columns of names. At the top of each column was a name in all capital letters with a date below it.

"Each of these," Jack pointed to one of the names in all capital letters, "is the host or hostess of the house party along with the date of the party. The guest list is beneath each."

"And what's this?" I asked.

Next to each date was an odd word or two. Some seemed almost normal while some were pure gibberish.

"The location. All in or very near Devon."

"Dunchideock Cross?" I stared at him.

"Yes. Lovely little inland parish."

"I see." I didn't, but I wasn't going to admit it. "It looks like Lady Antonia has only been to the first house party and this one. She did say she's been away to the South of France."

"Doesn't clear her," he said. "But it does make her unlikely."

"Agreed. Mr. Frain, Mary Parlance, and Lady Fortescue have been to all the parties... which doesn't look good for them."

"Although," Jack pointed out, "Simon Parlance missed one. And he and his sister never do anything on their own."

"Except go to house parties," I said dryly. "Alexander Malburn has been to three of the five, which puts him low on our list of suspects."

"Lord Chasterly himself has also been at all the parties save one. We can't leave him out."

"No," I agreed. "He's definitely on the suspect list, though why he'd steal from his peers and then ask Mr. Woodward for help is beyond me. As far as I can tell, he doesn't need the money."

"People don't always steal for the money," Jack reminded me.

"True. I worked with a woman during the war. Dolly. Kept stealing stupid little things. Items out of people's lunches or lockers, small tools, bits and pieces of scrap. She didn't need any of it, but she had some sort of condition. They had to let her go, though they at least didn't prosecute the poor woman. They could have since it was war time, but they brushed it under the rug, and we all pretended she'd gotten a better job offer."

"Poor woman. Must have been very unhappy."

I thought about it. "Actually, she seemed quite cheerful. She was sorry about it and returned everything she could, but otherwise, a very happy person. She just couldn't control her need to take things." I returned my focus to the list. "There are three names here that aren't on Lord Chasterly's guest list."

"Yes, Lady Olivander, Sir Ruben, and Vivian Morenton," he said. "But you missed these others." He tapped the list of five more names.

"Yes, but those were only each at one of the house parties in question and none were invited to Lord Chasterly's, so I think we can leave them out for now."

"I suppose you're right," he agreed.

"Tell me about these other three. Why aren't they on Lord Chasterly's guest list?" It seemed to me that, seeing as how they were at all the other parties, they *should* be on the list.

"He and Lady Olivander can't stand each other," Jack explained. "In fact, it was her party he missed."

"Really? Why?"

He squirmed uneasily. "Rumor has it that years ago they were... ah... close. *Very* close. If you know what I mean."

I frowned, wondering what he was getting at. Then it hit me, and I felt like a prize idiot. "Oh, you mean they were having an affair."

His eyes widened and his cheeks turned bright red, making him look kind of adorable. "Er, yes, rather. It all went sour, and the two have barely spoken since. Although, of course, they move in the same circles and are often at the same parties and such."

"But it would explain why she isn't on the guest list," I mused. "It does not, however, expunge her from the suspect list."

"Indeed not. Especially as, according to my uncle, she's been in a bit of a financial bind since her husband passed."

Now that was interesting, but it didn't necessarily mean anything. After all, she wasn't invited to this party.

"Now Sir Ruben actually is quite chummy with Lord Chasterly," Jack continued. "Sir Ruben is a bit older, but Lord Chasterly went to school with Sir Ruben's younger brother. They're also very distantly related."

"So why wouldn't he be invited?"

"I believe he was. Or at least my uncle is under that impression. Only he supposedly had to attend to some business or other in London and couldn't go, although he should be at the soiree over the weekend."

"I see." I tapped the pen against my chin. "Once again, that doesn't rule him out. He could quite easily take a train or drive from London. And then, of course, there's the shindig on Saturday."

"Very true, though once again motive isn't clear. He's extremely wealthy, and not just from family money. He made his own, you see. Hence the knighthood."

"Final name… Vivian Moreton. Who's she?"

He cleared his throat and his cheeks pinkened again. "She's an actress. Wouldn't usually be invited to such parties, but she's actually the daughter of a baron and not only rather wealthy, but exceptionally beautiful."

I felt an odd little stab of jealousy at the moony face he made. "Why wouldn't she be invited?"

"That I don't know," he admitted. "It's not like Lord Chasterly is the sort of stick in the mud to not invite her because of her profession. Although he is rather smitten with Lady Antonia, so perhaps he didn't want anyone else trying to steal her thunder, so to speak."

I couldn't imagine anyone stealing the limelight from Toni. Not only was she beautiful, but she had charisma in spades. I felt a bit like an ugly little sparrow next to a swan. Not that I minded. I'd never been one to crave the spotlight, but I did wish that men like Jack wouldn't moon over women just because they were exceptionally beautiful. Some of us had more important things. Like brains.

I reminded myself that I had a job to do and to stay on task. I cleared my throat. "I guess we should focus on just those who are at the house party, at least for now."

"Agreed, though I can do some checking on the other names, particularly those that were at all the other parties. Double check their alibis, so to speak."

"Good idea. We should know if one or more of them is in the neighborhood. That won't look good for them."

"Indeed not," Jack agreed. "So what is your plan?"

"I'm not sure," I admitted. "I've never been undercover before. And the only guest I've met so far is Lady Antonia. She seems very nice, but I don't suppose that means anything. I guess I'll simply have to meet each guest and determine my first impressions."

"And then?" he prodded.

I sighed. "Golly, I don't know. Listen to what they say? Though I suppose they won't talk about their plans to steal everyone's valuables. Maybe search their rooms? Although I doubt they'd have anything suspicious hidden yet."

"No, likely not. I suggest you keep your eyes and ears open and be prepared to search the moment anything is reported missing."

"In other words, investigate after the fact."

He shrugged. "It's really all we can do. Here." He reached beneath the table and passed me a velvet bag.

With some reluctance, I took it and peered inside. Something glittered back. Something that looked like diamonds. "What is this?"

"A brooch that belonged to my grandmother. My uncle thought it would be attractive to the thief."

I shook my head. "I couldn't bear it if it were to get stolen."

"That's rather the point," he said wryly. "Be sure and wear it where the other guests will see it. It's gauche to talk about the value of something, but you're American, so they'll expect it."

The remark both stung and angered, but I bit my tongue. "Very well. I'll do my best."

"You know what to do then?"

"Oh, yes," I said dryly. "I'm the bait."

Chapter 6

Tippy was still waiting patiently for me outside the pub. I was glad to be in the clean, fresh air, away from the smoke and the stares of the men inside. The wind whipped at my updo, loosening locks to dance around my cheeks.

"Perhaps we should stroll along the waterfront, Tippy," I said as I untied his leash. "Seems like a lovely day for it. Perhaps I can get a stamp from the post office. I really should send this letter to Mama."

I'd already sent my parents a letter from London explaining my surprising inheritance and its terms, as well as the fact that I had a new job. I did not explain my new job involved going under cover to catch a criminal but kept to the cover story of being Mr. Woodward's secretary. I knew it would likely come as quite a shock, especially since Mama had expected me back in Portland by now, but I was hoping she would understand and approve. After all, my mother had been something of an adventuress before she met my father.

Well, perhaps calling her an adventuress was a bit too far. But she had traveled all the way to New York City to visit a cousin who was in the theater. It was quite a scandal in the family. The cousin's profession, not my mother's visit. In fact, some of the relations refused to speak of her. Again, the cousin, not my mother. But Mama had spent a whole two months there and often told stories about all the people she'd met and the places she'd been. But only when my father wasn't listening. He didn't approve.

"Come, Tippy."

Tippy trotted alongside me, tongue lolling. His claws made little clippy sounds on the cobblestones.

I clutched my handbag tighter, remembering what was now inside. "Did you know that Jack and his uncle want to use me as bait?"

I swear Tippy's clever fox face held a little grin.

"Yes, you may find it amusing, but you're not the one who will have to face down a burglar. I'm finding this a little bit terrifying if you want to know the truth."

Tippy let out a soft woof. I'm not sure it was meant to be comforting, but I decided to take it that way. I also decided not to question the fact I was talking to a dog.

I paused to take in the stunning view. Gulls wheeled overhead as the ocean gently lapped against the sandy beach. It was low tide, but I could tell during high tide there would be no beach at all. The watermark came quite a way up the sea wall. Out on the water, little boats bobbed. Fishermen, no doubt. It was early yet, but I was betting they'd haul in their catch soon enough, and then the sleepy waterfront would be bustling and smelly. But for now, it was serene, the tang of saltwater heavy in the air.

The post office was just a block off the promenade in a lovely little stone building with a red door and red window sashes. The wooden door creaked, and a brass bell tinkled as I entered. There were only two people inside and they both turned to stare at me.

Both women were middle aged and wore simple, boxy shaped dresses popular during the lean years of the war, in direct contrast to my Christian Dior with its longer hemline and full, swishy skirt. A spark of embarrassment flooded me that I was frivolously flaunting my wealth. Which was ridiculous. I wasn't at all wealthy, but everyone was supposed to think I was.

The woman on my side of the counter wore a blue dress—the floral fabric faded with use, clearly the result of many washings—with stout, low-heeled brown shoes and a well-worn brown mac. She held a shopping bag and an oversized brown handbag in one hand and had been gesticulating wildly with the other. At least until I walked in.

The woman behind the counter was stouter than her companion, and while I couldn't see her shoes, her dress was a vivid pink, although mostly covered with a yellow apron. Her graying hair was held off her face with a matching swatch of pink fabric.

I felt completely out of place. Would a wealthy aristocrat buy her own stamps?

Probably not. But I was American, so even if one of Lord Chasterly's guests stumbled across my gauche behavior, they'd probably chalk it up to that.

"Can I help you, miss?" the woman behind the counter asked, giving me a thorough once-over.

"Yes. I'd like to mail this letter to America." I placed the envelope on the counter, giving the woman in the blue dress an apologetic look.

"Ah, of course. You must be up at the Big House."

Since Aunt Euphegenia's cottage was anything but big, I could only assume she meant Endmere, I nodded. "Yes, Lord Chasterly is such a wonderful host." I told myself to shut up. I seemed to be blabbing needlessly.

The postmistress smiled warmly. "Well, I hope you enjoy your stay. I'm Mrs. Johnson. If you need anything, just let me know."

Her kindness made me relax just a little. "Sugar Martin."

The woman in the blue dress snorted. "Whatever kind of name is that?"

"Margeret, don't be rude," Mrs. Johnson, snapped. "Don't mind her, love."

I swear Margeret tilted her nose ever so slightly and sniffed. "That your dog?"

I glanced down. Tippy had followed me in. Or rather, I'd brought him in since I'd forgotten to tie him up outside. "Oh, yes. Sorry. I should have left him outside."

"Pish posh," said Mrs. Johnson. "He's fine. How odd. He looks a lot like—well, no it can't be."

I had a bad feeling she recognized him, so I quickly changed the subject. "Are you by any chance related to the butler at Endmere?"

She took the letter and sat it gently on a scale. "He's my brother-in-law. That'll be fifteen pee."

My mind scrambled. Pee? I wasn't sure what that meant. I opened my handbag, pulled out my coin purse, and scrambled inside, trying to figure it out.

"Pence," Margeret said slowly as if I was stupid. "Pee is short for pence."

"Of course." My laugh sounded as strained and awkward as I felt. I counted out fifteen pence and handed it to the woman behind the counter.

The women took up their conversation again as my letter was appropriately stamped and placed into the right slot, and my receipt was written up. It seemed a Mr. Higgins was a bit of a lout, and a drunken one at that, and it was too bad as his wife was lovely. Also, the sermon on Sunday had gone on a bit long and someone ought to talk to the vicar about it. Finally, little Tommy Tilbury had been done—I gathered that meant he'd been arrested—for stealing Mrs. Potts's prized chicken, but it had only been a prank, so he'd been let off with only a warning after an hour in a cell.

"Speaking of thefts," I found myself blurting, "have you heard about the robberies?" I wanted to wilt into the floor as two pairs of eyes swung my way.

"Robberies?" Mrs. Johnson echoed.

"What robberies?" Margeret asked, small eyes shrewd. She had clearly spotted a tasty bit of gossip.

I swallowed and dove in. "Well, as you know, I'm staying at Lord Chasterly's. He's having a house party this weekend."

They both nodded, gazes glued to my face.

I cleared my throat. "I've been hearing from the other guests that other house parties in the area have been robbed. Valuable items stolen. Some right out of the guests' rooms while they're sleeping."

"You don't say!" Mrs. Johnson leaned on the counter, making a shelf for her ample bosom. "What sort of valuables?"

"Antique brooches, diamond cocktail rings, pearls, that sort of thing," I said.

Margeret's eyes were glittering with barely suppressed excitement. "Do you know who was robbed?"

Apparently, the names of the wealthy and titled victims were a hotter commodity than the items themselves. "Ah, not exactly. But I believe Lord Chasterly himself had a gold money clip stolen, along with a small amount of cash."

Margeret let out a sound that was downright gleeful. "Were the robbers armed?"

"I have no idea," I admitted. "It always happened when people were either asleep, or away from the house so no one ever saw the thief. They don't even know if it's one person or several."

"How exciting!" Margeret exclaimed.

"Not for those that lost their valuables, I reckon," Mrs. Johnson said dryly. "Afraid this is the first I've heard of such a thing. My brother-in-law keeps things close to the vest. Very uppity that one."

"Well, they're trying to keep it hush hush," I said. "Not wanting news to get out. Doesn't look good or something. Where I come from, they'd have the full police force out, combing the countryside."

"That's because Americans aren't so uptight about appearances," Mrs. Johnson said without rancor. "The upper classes here, they want everyone to think they're untouchable."

Margeret nodded. "True enough."

"I'm a little worried someone will target this house party," I admitted.

"Not to worry." Mrs. Johnson patted my hand. "If we hear anything or see anything suspicious, we'll let you know."

"Would you? That would be so kind of you." I doubted they would, but it wouldn't hurt to have the locals keeping an eye out. Especially since, soon enough, they would be my neighbors.

Hopefully they wouldn't be too upset by my keeping them in the dark about that.

After a few more pleasantries, and a whine from Tippy, we were on our way, bidding Mrs. Johnson and Margeret goodbye.

"They were nice," I said to Tippy. "At least Aunt Euphegenia's cottage is in such a lovely, peaceful town."

Tippy let out an ungentlemanly snort.

Chapter 7

When I arrived back at Endmere, a long, black car sat in the drive. Johnson was supervising the extraction of several pieces of luggage from the trunk—or boot, as the British called it.

"Miss Martin, you've been walking," he said with a faint tone of disapproval.

"Of course," I said merrily. "It's such a lovely day, and I wanted to explore a bit. Plus Tippy needed some exercise."

Tippy shot me a glare, which was hard to do since his tongue was lolling out the side of his mouth. He was surprisingly cute.

"If you would leave the dog with me, I will ensure he is watered. Lady Fortescue has arrived, and everyone is having pre-luncheon cocktails in the drawing room."

Pre-lunch cocktails? It wasn't even five o'clock! What sort of rabbit hole had I fallen down?

I handed Tippy over to Johnson and dashed up the stairs to wash my hands, refresh my powder and lipstick, and pat my rather windblown hair into place. I figured my simple afternoon dress was good enough for lunch—though I did attach the brooch Jack had loaned me—and dashed back down.

Outside the drawing room, I took a deep breath to steady my nerves before stepping inside. I immediately relaxed a bit as I saw that, in addition to Lord Chasterly, there was only Lady Antonia and one other woman.

The newcomer was tall, angular, with bottle blonde hair cut into a rather severe bob that would have been more in place fifteen years ago, as would the Japanese style dress which hugged her form. Still, it all looked rather good on her.

"Ah, Sugar!" Lord Chasterly boomed. "Come meet the other guests. Martini?"

"Um, sure." I took the proffered glass and sniffed at it gingerly. I swear it singed the ends of my nose hairs.

"Ladies, this is Sugar Martin, friend of the family."

It was the first I'd heard of it, but I smiled and nodded as if Freddy and I had known each other for ages.

"Sugar, this is the Countess of Netherford, but we mostly call her Lady Antonia."

"Call me Toni," Lady Antonia said, pretending we hadn't just met in the middle of the night. She gave me a vigorous shake and a knowing wink as if to say, "Play along, chum."

"And this," Lord Chasterly turned to the blonde woman, "is Lady Fortescue."

As if not to be outdone by Toni, Lady Fortescue also gave me a hearty handshake and a booming, "Call me Lil."

"Pleased to meet you both," I said, retrieving my hand and hiding behind my Martini glass. Liquid courage was just what I needed, singed nose hairs or not.

"The rest of the guests will arrive in time for supper," Lord Chasterly answered my unspoken question. "In the meantime, we'll do jolly well without them, shan't we ladies?" His jovial smile, while given to all of us, was clearly meant for Toni.

Lil gave the other woman a sour look before turning back to me. "Sugar. That's an *unusual* name." She said "unusual" as if she smelled fish that had just gone off.

I smiled tightly, unsure how to answer. If I told her my name was Euphegenia, would she connect it with my aunt and thus realize I wasn't an heiress at all? Instead, I said, "My father always called me Sugar."

She smiled tightly. "How... quaint."

I disliked her immediately and almost as strongly as I'd liked Toni. Whereas Toni was free-spirited, cheerful, and kind, Lil was uptight, arrogant, and—frankly—a bit of a pill.

It was clear to me that while Lil was sweet on Lord Chasterly, good ole Freddy was far more interested in Toni. Meanwhile, Toni didn't give a fig. She was more interested in her Martini and in regaling me with tales of her latest trip to Paris where she'd "swung by" after her months on the French Riviera.

"It was *divine,* darling. You'd hardly know there'd been a war on. Well, alright, there's a bit of a mess here and there," she admitted. "But it wasn't nearly as badly hit as London, and it's still beautiful even if parts are in a bit of a shambles. The men are still delicious, and there are great deals to be had on designer clothing if you know where to go."

I smiled and nodded, again unsure of what to say. The only attack on the U.S. mainland during World War II was the bombing of Fort Stevens on the Oregon Coast in June of 1942. Despite the Japanese firing seventeen missiles at the fort, nobody was hurt, and the only real damage caused was the severing of a few telephone wires. Needless to say, it did cause everyone quite a scare and rolls of barbed wire were strung along the coast for the duration of the war. Fortunately, they were never needed.

Meanwhile, entire European cities were smashed into oblivion by the *Luftwaffe* or the Royal Air Force, depending on which side they were on. Thousands of civilians had died. I didn't feel I had the right to comment on what Paris or anywhere else looked like.

"You're from America," Lil drawled. "Which part?"

"Oregon," I said.

"Where's that? Anywhere near Hollywood?" Lil asked.

"About a thousand miles away," I said rather dryly.

Lil raised her brow but didn't say anything. I got the distinct impression that in her mind, if it wasn't Hollywood or New York, it didn't exist. It was an attitude with which I was familiar.

There was a great crash from the hall accompanied by furious barking and a shouted, "Tippy!"

The next moment, Tippy strutted into the room—that was the only word for it—dragging his leash behind him. Nose in the air, he made a beeline for the hearth and heaved himself down with a gusty sigh.

Penny arrived next, her neat uniform covered in mud and her ginger bun askew. A twig was caught in her curls, one stocking was torn at the knee, and she was panting like a freight train.

"Oh, dear, what did he do?" I shot Tippy a glare.

Tippy merely sniffed.

"Sorry, my lord, my ladies," Penny said between puffs. "But he got away from me."

"Did he break anything?" I asked, recalling the terrible crash.

"No, miss. Just knocked over the silver tray Johnson uses to collect the post. Oh, and that brass vase with the lilies in it. But everything seems to have survived."

I breathed a sigh of relief. I personally didn't have the funds to replace anything Tippy broke, and I doubted Mr. Woodward would be pleased if he had to pony up. He might decide to take it out of my wages.

"Why don't you run along, Penny," Lord Chasterly said cheerfully. "Let Tippy take his nap by the fire. He isn't bothering anyone."

"Of course, my lord. I'll just get his leash."

Tippy eyed Penny with mistrust the entire time, but once the leash was free and she had disappeared out the door, he closed his eyes. In no time he was snoring away.

Before we could return to our conversation, there was another hubbub in the hall and a young-ish man poked his nose in the door. "All here?"

"Raymond!" Lord Chasterly all but shouted. "Come on in, old chap. Have a cocktail."

This, then, was Raymond of the indecipherable last name. He was very ordinary looking—average height, average build, average looks. He'd an impressive Roman nose and a prominent Adam's apple. His hair was a dull mousy brown and seemed to be trying to vacate the vicinity of his face. Meanwhile, his eyebrows were trying to make up for it as they bushed out wildly in all directions like drunken caterpillars. His brown suit neither fit properly nor suited his coloring.

Lord Chasterly handed him a cocktail and was about to make introductions when two more people entered the room. Whereas Raymond had been quiet and reticent, appearing out of place and awkward, these two swanned in like they owned the manor. They were about as opposite in looks from poor Raymond as one could imagine.

It was like looking at two sides of a coin, male and female. They appeared to be in their early twenties. Both were blond and stunningly good looking with the sort of golden-tanned skin one only gets in places like California or

Greece. Their eyes were identical cornflower blue with identical dark, perfectly arched brows and thick, sweeping lashes. They were dressed in the height of fashion to show off athletic figures. Since they could only be brother and sister, I had to assume they were Simon and Mary Parlance.

Mary greeted Lord Chasterly with a cheek kiss while he and Simon shook hands energetically. Once they'd been supplied with cocktails, Freddy made the introductions.

I at last discovered that Raymond's surname was Frain. Apparently, while he was a simple "Mister," Simon and Mary were "Honorables" as Penny had mentioned in her note (Although she'd spelled it with a "u" which I could only guess was a British spelling). Whatever that meant. I'd no idea how to address them properly. Fortunately, Mary rescued me by assuring me I was to call them by their given names.

"We're all among friends, here," she said lightly, taking a sip of her cocktail. "Oh, Freddy, darling, these are marvelous! What do you call them?"

"The Singapore Sling, love." He'd swapped out the martinis for some fruity concoction. "Haven't you had one before? I picked up the recipe years ago when I was visiting the Far East."

As the rest of the guests chatted among themselves, I took stock. It appeared we were only missing Alexander Malburn. I wondered how he'd fit into this motley crew. They all seemed so mismatched.

Since Mr. Frain was standing by himself, I wandered over and gave him one of my award-winning smiles. Not that I'd ever won an award, mind you, but my mother has always said I have a very nice smile, and I always could wrap my father around my little finger if I gave him my most winsome one.

"You're Mr. Frain, right?" I said, simply to strike up conversation.

"Er, quite. But you can call me Raymond." He took a huge gulp of his drink as if those few words had drained him and he needed to refortify himself.

"And I'm Sugar."

"Interesting name," he all but muttered, his ears going crimson.

I figured he must be incredibly shy. "What is it you do, Raymond?"

That startled a laugh out of him. "That's a bit cheeky of you."

"Oh, sorry, did I faux pas?" I asked, suddenly feeling a bit embarrassed. Why had Mr. Woodward thought sending me was a good idea? I was sure to stick my foot in it more than once.

"Well, usually among these sorts of people," he waved a hand to indicate the rest of the guests, "one doesn't talk about how one makes money. It's considered common."

"Oh. Oh, dear. I'm afraid it's quite a normal thing in the U.S. to speak about what one does for a living."

"Is it?" That piqued his interest.

"Yes. You see, one's chosen field can say a lot about one's interests," I said. "Or not. I admit I was a much better welder than secretary."

"Really? Do tell."

Oh, damnation. I was supposed to be an heiress! "Oh, I don't want to bother you with the boring details."

"Never," he assured me. "You see, to answer your question, I'm a writer. So I find people's stories to be most interesting."

A writer? Amongst Freddy's fancy friends? How astonishing! "Oh, well, if that's the case... during the war, I worked at the shipyards in Portland. That's my hometown. The men were all off to fight, but somebody had to build ships for the Navy, so they hired us women. Asked what we were interested in. Seemed I had a knack for welding. I'd have stayed on after the war was over, but the boys came home and, well, they needed jobs. Didn't matter that I was a better welder than any of them."

"So you became a secretary instead?"

"Oh, yes. A more acceptable job for a woman." There may have been some sarcasm in my tone. "But I was terrible at it. I'm a very slow typist, I can't do shorthand to save my life, and I kept accidentally hanging up on people when I tried to transfer calls to my boss."

He chuckled. "It sounds like secretarial positions are not your calling."

"No indeed," I agreed whole heartedly. "The worst was my last position. I worked for a toy company."

"How interesting."

"You'd think," I said dryly. "But I worked with a lot of men who were, to put it bluntly, not terribly bright and kind of boorish. One pinched my bottom." I winced, Unsure why I'd told him that.

His eyes widened. "What did you do?"

I shrugged. "I slugged him in the kisser. Needless to say, I was promptly unemployed."

He let out a surprisingly hearty guffaw. "Well, it served the man right. Too bad you had to pay for it. What do you do now?"

I froze a moment before letting out a tittering laugh. "Why, I'm an heiress, haven't you heard? I'm surprised one of the others didn't tell you. My aunt, or rather great-aunt, died recently and left me a fortune."

That was putting it rather strongly. Aunt Euphegenia had left a nice sum, but it wasn't exactly a fortune. Not to mention she'd left it to her dog.

"So no more playing secretary. Bully for you!" He raised his glass in a toast and offered me a wide smile that turned his plain face into something almost bordering handsome.

He was a nice fellow. I really hoped he wasn't the thief. I was still trying to figure out how to worm the whole burglary thing into conversation when we were called to dinner by Johnson pounding on a gong.

"Mr. Malburn sends his apologies, my lord, but he's running late and won't be here until early morning tomorrow."

"Typical Alex," Freddy said cheerfully, taking Toni's arm to lead her into dinner.

That, of course, left Lil glaring at them. It seemed Toni outranked Lil or something like that, so the host had to escort her. The whole thing was equal nonsense and rather charming.

Freddy played host at one end of the table while Toni sat in for hostess at the other, which naturally made Lil see green, though she did settle down when she discovered she was seated next to Freddy. I was seated between Simon Parlance and the empty chair that was supposed to include Alex Malburn. Raymond Frain sat across from me with Mary next to him.

"Come sit by me, Sugar," Toni begged. "We can have a bit of girl talk."

I'd hoped to have a chance to question Raymond further and perhaps Simon as well, but this would maybe give me the chance to bond with Mary and find out what she knew.

Plus, I enjoyed Toni's company, so I scooted over a seat.

Dinner was a jovial affair of five courses, starting with something Toni informed me was a consommé burnoise. To me, it looked like a lot of neatly diced vegetables in a clear broth, also referred to as vegetable soup. It more or less tasted like that, too, only perhaps richer than what my mother cooked on her stove at home.

Next came large chunks of fish accompanied by a gravy boat of Hollandaise sauce.

"Poached turbot!" Toni declared, clapping her hands. "How lovely."

I took only a small portion, already feeling a bit full from the soup and not being a huge fan of fish. Although I do love a good prawn, and I have a feeling if I ever get the chance to taste lobster, I'll love that, too.

The third course was of roast guinea fowl which Lord Chasterly informed us he'd shot himself. I hoped I didn't chip a tooth on a stray piece of buckshot, but it was surprisingly tasty, meaty, if a bit gamey.

When dessert arrived, I was hoping it was the last course. I was already feeling overstuffed, but the raspberry fool—fresh raspberries whipped into a rich vanilla custard and topped with more fresh raspberries—looked divine and tasted better.

And then the final course arrived, and I nearly let out a groan as the cheese platter was passed around. Frankly, I didn't understand why they were eating cheese *after* dessert. It seemed a bit... backward.

By the time we regrouped in the sitting room for coffee and cognac, I was swearing off food. This was nuts. Wasn't Britain on rations?

When I said so to Toni she laughed. "Darling, look at this place. Do you think Freddy has to worry about a bit of rationing? Not to mention, fish isn't rationed. In any case, just about everything we ate came from this property, except the sugar, of course, but he's got bees so there's plenty of honey."

It was astonishing to me that one could have so much food during a time when it was supposedly scarce. It simply baffled. If I ate like this every day, none of my new dresses would fit.

The after-dinner conversation was incredibly dull. Everyone gossiping about people

I'd never heard of and places I'd never been. I was about to excuse myself—after all, I was feeling tired, not being used to such late hours—when the conversation suddenly took an interesting turn.

"Did you ever find your necklace, Lil?" Simon asked loudly.

Everyone turned to stare at her.

Lil's expression was clearly one of anger and frustration. "No, I haven't. I'm telling you the thief took it at Lady Harwood's garden party. I know it. And it was an heirloom, too!"

I realized they were referring to one of the thefts by the mysterious house party burglar. I perked up, hoping to learn something interesting.

"I'm sure they'll catch him eventually," Freddy soothed. "Maybe they'll be able to recover your necklace then."

"What do you suppose they'll do to the thief once they catch him?" Toni mused.

Lil's face was growing redder by the minute. "I hope they hang him."

Shéa MacLeod

Chapter 8

"Come now, that seems a bit much, old girl," Freddy said as everyone else stared at Lil in shock.

I could understand being upset about a stolen heirloom. Even wanting the person responsible to pay. But wanting them to hang? That seemed a bit over the top. I made a personal note to never get on Lil's bad side.

"I don't think so at all," she said, her cheeks reddening. "These people, they take advantage. How dare they think they have a right to take what isn't theirs. They should pay!"

"I agree," Mary said with a tipsy giggle. "To making them pay!" She raised her glass in mock salute.

"What would you do if you ran into burglar?" Simon asked Lil curiously. He seemed completely unperturbed by her outburst.

"Why, I'd bash him on the head with a fire poker," she said.

It sounded like she meant it. Good grief, these people were bloodthirsty. Or at least Lil was. Everyone else seemed to laugh it off except for Raymond Frain who looked unaccountably nervous. Then a look came over his face, one of understanding as if a lightbulb had just gone off. I swear I heard him mutter, "That would be too easy."

Interesting. Could he then be the thief? Or perhaps know something about the burglaries? Or maybe he was simply referring to something he was writing.

I decided to ask him about it as soon as possible but didn't get a chance. He excused himself early and disappeared to his room. Since the rest were getting increasingly drunk and loud, I, too, excused myself, though I took a detour on the way to my room.

Raymond's room was down the hall perpendicular to mine, but the light was already off. I hesitated, then decided I could always speak to him in the morning.

I found Tippy snoozing on the bed.

"No dogs on the furniture, Tippy!" I shooed him off, and he gave me a very dirty look for it. A look which I completely ignored.

My room was overly warm and smelled a bit of dog, so I opened the window and let in the fresh spring breeze. The air was redolent with the sweetness of wisteria. A night bird called to its mate while in the distance a train whistled mournfully. Still, my brain was too busy trying to work out what was going on with Lil, Raymond, the burglaries. It took forever to fall asleep, but at last I nodded off.

It felt like I'd only been asleep mere minutes when I started awake. A glance at the clock showed it was six in the morning. The sky was just turning that gunmetal gray right before dawn and a bird was singing an annoyingly incessant five notes over and over. Except that wasn't what woke me up. It wasn't what had my heart racing against my ribcage.

Tippy stood, lips pulled back, ears pointed. A slight growl emerged from his throat. Whatever it was had disturbed him as well.

Groggily, I tried to recall what it was. A scream. Someone had screamed.

"What's wrong?" a male voice shouted from up the hall. I thought it was Simon.

"I heard a scream." A woman's voice this time. I had no idea which one.

I staggered out of bed, snagged my bathrobe, and shrugged it on. I didn't bother with slippers despite the chilly floor. I was used to going barefoot. With Tippy hot on my heels, I hurried out the door.

Simon and his sister stood at the head of the stairs staring down into the foyer below. They turned at my approach.

"You heard it, too," Mary said. Even without makeup and her hair under a kerchief, she was stunningly beautiful.

I nodded. "Do you know what happened?"

They both shook their heads in unison. It was kind of creepy.

I started down the stairs with Tippy leading the way, the Parlance siblings reluctantly following. I wondered where the others were and who it was who'd screamed. And why?

Tippy aimed straight for the sitting room. There was a single light on, and the embers glowed orange in the fireplace. I immediately spotted Lady Antonia perched on the edge of a settee still wearing last night's dress, her hair mussed as if she'd fallen asleep on the couch. She stared into the coals, her face a mask, as if she'd seen a ghost.

And there, lying on the rug face down next to the fire was a man. He wasn't moving.

Tippy trotted over and sniffed at him. Still he didn't move.

"Tippy, get away from there," I said, my voice sounding tight and frightened even to myself. Why wasn't the man moving? I felt a sort of sick dread, a tightness in my throat. Still, I forced myself forward. "Toni, what is it? What's wrong?"

She didn't answer. She just started rocking back and forth. Shock. I'd seen it before when one of the welding girls was injured. Burned herself pretty horribly. But Toni didn't look injured.

I swallowed hard. "Tippy, go sit with Toni."

Tippy whined, but trotted over to Toni and sat, his chin resting on her knee. She absentmindedly stroked his head, and he let out a little doggy sound of ecstasy.

"Who is it?" Simon asked from behind me.

"I don't know," I admitted. The man was dressed in a bathrobe which had come undone and spread out, partially hiding his build.

"Is he dead?" Mary asked.

"I don't know," I repeated, annoyed. Why was I the one being asked these questions?

"Well, why don't you check his pulse?" Simon suggested.

I shot him a glare over my shoulder. What a wimp.

Swallowing my own trepidation, I knelt down next to the body and felt for a pulse. Nothing. But then I wasn't exactly used to taking pulses, so I turned his head in order to check his breath. I gasped. "It's Raymond Frain."

"Jeepers," Simon said, although I notice he didn't seem surprised. His expression was as calm and unruffled as ever.

I held my hand in front of Raymond's nose, but there was nothing. No hint of breath. And in dim light I realized that on one side of his head his hair was sticky and matted. A dark stain spread out into the pale carpet under him, as if he'd been bleeding.

"I think he's dead," I said through stiff lips.

Mary let out a gasp and Simon muttered something that sounded like a word that shouldn't be said in polite company. Toni didn't even blink; she just kept stroking Tippy's fur.

And then I saw it, lying there so innocently. A poker.

I'd smash him in the head with a poker.

My mouth went dry. "We need to call the police."

"I don't believe it." Lord Chasterly ran a hand through his thick hair. It looked to me like his hand might be shaking a little.

We were currently gathered in the dining room while the police inspected the crime scene. Crime scene? Good heavens, how shocking! I was definitely going to leave this out of my next letter home, or Mama would be jumping on the next airplane.

Johnson had served everyone coffee, although many of us were drinking something stronger. Even I had downed a bit of brandy. For the shock, you know.

"I'm sorry," I whispered. "I should have figured this out sooner. Maybe he'd still be alive."

"Nonsense," Freddy said bracingly, pulling me away from everyone. "You just got here. How were you supposed to figure anything out?"

He had a point. Not only that, but the rest of the guests, save one, had arrived mere hours ago. I'd nothing to go on. No one who'd roused my suspicions except the man who lay dead in the sitting room.

"I can't believe someone killed Raymond Frain," I said. "Do you suppose he could have been... well, you know?"

Freddy shook his head mournfully. "He must have been, mustn't he? Why else would anyone kill the poor chap?"

Well, I could think of a number of reasons one person might kill another, but in Raymond's case, I didn't want to speculate. I simply hadn't known him well enough. But there was the one glaringly obvious reason.

"Did he need money?" I kept my voice low knowing that the British considered talk of money vulgar. And also there was the whole under cover thing to consider.

"I know his last book didn't do as well as he'd hoped," Freddy admitted. "Recently he'd been a bit hard up. Didn't make much during the war, and his older brother inherited everything when their father died. Wouldn't even give him a loan. He was counting on his latest release to get him in the black again, but..." He shrugged.

"So things were tight. Was he the sort of person who'd do something illegal if he was desperate?"

Freddy mulled it over. "He'd have to have been even more desperate than I realized. And he would never hurt anyone or steal from anyone who couldn't afford the loss."

Which would explain why only the wealthy had been hit. Raymond had probably considered that those of his friends who spent their time lounging around at house parties dining like kings would hardly miss a bauble or two.

"It isn't looking good for the old chap, is it?" Freddy asked.

"I'm afraid not," I admitted. "But the question is, who killed him and why? Why here? Why tonight?"

"Maybe one of my other guests caught him in the act," he said.

"Possible, except why not just admit it?" Then, recalling the previous evening, I said, "Unless it was Lil. She did, after all, threaten to beat the thief to death with a poker."

"And that's just how he died!" Freddy looked aghast.

Not that I blamed him. He'd known these people for ages. It would be shocking to discover that one of your friends was capable of murder. And Lil certainly struck me as being capable. But had she done it?

A smooth-shaven man in a cheap navy suit appeared in the doorway and cleared his throat. All heads swiveled his direction.

"I am Detective Chief Inspector Cobblepot."

I nearly snickered, but managed to hold it in. No one else seemed to think it was funny.

"Now, before I ask your whereabouts and such, is everyone present and accounted for?"

Cobblepot asked, tapping his pencil against his little black notepad.

Everyone glanced around and Freddy said, "We're all here, Detective Chief Inspector, except the staff. They are gathered in the kitchen."

Cobblepot nodded. "Good. Good. Now, is anything missing from the house?"

There were gasps and mutterings, and then once again Freddy spoke up. "I apologize, DCI Cobblepot, but we never thought to check."

"Can you check now please? Everyone," Cobblepot said. "And come straight back here once you've had a look. No one is to leave the premises."

While Freddy had Johnson round up the servants to check the house, the rest of us went to our rooms. Mine was entirely undisturbed, save Tippy who gave me an annoyed look when I roused him from his perch on the window seat.

"I don't suppose anyone snuck in here without you knowing, did they?" I said.

He whined a little. I was taking that as a solid no, but I looked around anyway just in case. And then, conscious I was still in my nightclothes and slippers, I took the chance to make sure at least my hair looked halfway presentable and my teeth were brushed.

I was about to return to the dining room when I stopped. "Oh, dear." I rushed to the wardrobe and pulled out the dress I'd been wearing the previous evening. The one I'd pinned Jack's brooch to. It wasn't there.

I scrambled around the bottom of the wardrobe to see if it had fallen off. Nothing. I felt positively sick to my stomach. What was I going to tell Jack?

I was the first back downstairs and poked my head into the dining room. I was still debating whether or not to report the theft when the detective chief inspector stepped in front of me.

"Anything missing, Miss...?" Cobblepot prompted.

"Miss Martin. Miss Sugar Martin."

His brows went up.

I heaved a sigh. "Euphegenia, that's my first name, but everyone calls me Sugar."

He nodded and jotted it down in his notebook. "American?"

"Yes. And I checked my room. Nothing's missing." The lie slid off my tongue. I don't know why I didn't tell him the truth.

"Very good." He jotted something else. "When did you arrive?"

"Day before yesterday by train from London. I was the first to arrive." I didn't mention the real reason I was there.

"How do you know Lord Chasterly?"

"Family friend," I lied glibly. It wasn't entirely untruthful. After all, he was the friend of my great-aunt's solicitor.

"I see." More scribbles. "Where were you at between midnight and three?"

"Is that when he died?"

"Answer the question, Miss Martin," he said through gritted teeth.

"I was in bed asleep."

His pencil scratched against paper. "And how do you know the deceased?"

"I only met him when he arrived last evening. We had a brief discussion about his books—I discovered he was a writer—and that was about it. He seemed a nice man, if a little sad."

Cobblepot eyed me but didn't comment. "Very well. Thank you, Miss Martin."

"There is another thing," I said, trying not to feel guilty for ratting on Lil.

He sighed heavily. "What is it?"

I took him by the elbow and steered him into the room, away from the door, keeping my voice low. "We were all in the sitting room having drinks after dinner, and the topic of the house party robberies came up. You know about them?"

"I've heard." His tone was long-suffering.

"Well, one of the guests, Lady Fortescue, said that if she ever ran into the thief, she would beat him to death. With a poker."

This caught Cobblepot's attention. He stopped scribbling, and his shrewd gaze fell on me. "She did, did she?"

"Yes," I said. "She did. Now, it may have just been one of those silly things people say in anger. 'I could wring your neck' — that sort of thing. But I thought you should know."

"Thank you, Miss Martin, you've been very helpful." Although his tone said otherwise. He turned and beckoned to the uniformed officer standing guard by the door.

Clearly, I was being dismissed. I debated for a split second telling him the whole truth about Woodward hiring me to investigate, then decided against it. I didn't fancy having him laugh in my face.

"The others are in the library, Miss," the officer said as he showed me out.

"Thank you."

I had no intention of heading to the library. I wanted to see if I could get another look at the crime scene. Unfortunately, the officer insisted on walking with me, so I had no choice but to go along.

Sure enough, they were all sitting in the library, most with drinks in their hands. They glanced up as we entered.

"Lady Fortescue, if you will come with me?" the young officer said.

She rolled her eyes. "If I must."

While she joined him, I went to sit next to Toni. Maybe she would have some gossip.

"What'd I miss?" I asked, taking the chair next to her.

"Not much. Lil has been complaining non-stop about the inconvenience. As if poor Raymond wasn't far more inconvenienced by being murdered." She took a drag on her cigarette then stubbed it out in a crystal ashtray. "I really need to stop. Filthy habit."

I was in complete agreement on that but didn't say so. "Does anyone have anything missing?"

"Well, Lil claims a bracelet is missing, but the police didn't find it or anything else on Raymond."

Which meant they hadn't found Jack's brooch either. "Either he isn't the thief—"

"Or more likely Lil is lying," Toni interrupted, pulling out another cigarette then shoving it back in its case. She tapped her long red nails nervously on the silver case.

"Why would she lie?" I didn't bother mentioning the third possibility. That Raymond had an accomplice. That was something I needed to mull over a bit, but it fit.

Toni waved her hand as if to brush away an annoying insect. "Lil is always terribly dramatic. Comes from disappointment, I suppose."

"What do you mean?"

Her eyes glittered and she leaned in, clearly excited to share juicy gossip with someone from outside the usual circle. "She was engaged before the war. Devastatingly handsome young man, very heroic. Title, money, everything."

"What happened?"

"He died, darling. Like so many young men. He was a fighter pilot, and you know how *they* fared."

Not well. I felt a stab of empathy for Lil. I, too, knew what it was to lose one's beloved to war. "How sad for her."

"It was," Toni admitted. "We were all very sorry. She was devastated of course. And then his younger brother inherited everything... title, money, house. Everything that should have been hers was now the domain of his shrewish wife. Being the second son, no one had expected him to inherit, so their father hadn't objected when he married the daughter of a mere knight. Lil considers the woman common. Well, everybody does really, but now she's lady of the manor, and poor Lil has nothing."

"I thought she had money of her own," I said.

Toni snorted. "Hardly. Her brother gives her a small stipend, and she's allowed to use the family's London house, but nothing is *hers*, and her brother's wife constantly lords it over her. She's very bitter about it. Lil, I mean—not the wife."

I could see how it would be a hard pill to swallow. Going from the expectation of a life of luxury and position to having to take handouts from family. "I guess she never found anyone else."

"Oh, there were a few proposals, at least in the early days, but none of them were good enough for her." Toni shook her head. "But look where her pride has got her."

I leaned in and whispered, "Is it true she's in love with Freddy?"

Toni gave me a shrewd look. "You don't miss much, do you? I don't know about love so much as she's set her cap for him. Properly titled, plenty of money, and possibly her last chance. She's not getting any younger."

"Except he's clearly not interested," I said, my pity for the woman growing by the minute.

"Not even a little," Toni said. "But don't feel too sorry for her. Her own pride and bitterness has been her downfall. If she hadn't been so uppity, she might have found happiness."

"Is that what you did?" I could have bit my tongue. I knew Toni to be a widow.

But she wasn't angry. She laughed. "Oh, you are a delight. In fact, no. I didn't marry for love. I married for money. Loads of it." She winked.

I wasn't sure whether she was pulling my leg or not. Oh, I was certain she was telling the truth about having lots of money, but I wasn't sure if that was her reason for marrying in the first place, and I suddenly felt unable to pry further.

There was a commotion out in the hall, and Lil stormed past, marching up the stairs. Cobblepot appeared in the doorway, shaking his head. He opened his mouth, but before he could speak, there was a shriek.

Almost as one, we stormed up the stairs behind her. The door to Lil's room was open, and she stood in the middle of the room, staring around her in horror. The place was a mess, clothes tossed everywhere, cosmetic pots tipped over, nail varnish dripping down the side of the vanity. And along one wall, scrawled in red, the word DIE.

We all stared, transfixed.

An unfamiliar masculine voice piped up from behind me, "Hey. What'd I miss?"

Chapter 9

"Who the devil are you?" Cobblepot demanded, his wild eyebrows growing wilder by the minute. "Constable! Detain this man!"

"Hey!" The newcomer held up his hands in surrender. "What's going on? I just got here."

"Alex." Freddy wended his way through the crowd and gave the stranger a manly handshake. "You've stepped into a hornet's nest, my good fellow, that's for sure."

"Do tell," Alex said cheerfully.

This then was Alexander Malburn, the missing guest. He was exceedingly handsome, although perhaps not as handsome as Simon Parlance, with hair the color of a raven's wing in loose ringlets about his head and unusually large eyes—the same gray as a Pacific Northwest raincloud—ringed by sooty lashes. His nose was perfectly straight, but his lips were a little fuller than most British men and his skin, while pale, held just a hint of duskiness as if he had perhaps a touch of Roman or Moroccan blood.

He wore a casual but expensive navy suit with a pale blue button-down shirt and a wide yellow and blue tie. His driving loafers looked like they might be Italian leather, and he carried a fedora in one hand. Every inch the gentleman of wealth and leisure.

"Detective Inspector." Freddy turned to Cobblepot. "This is my good friend, Mr. Alexander Malburn. He was meant to come down last night but was delayed. Isn't that right, dear boy?"

"Sure thing," Alex said with a movie-star grin. "Had a bit of business to attend to in London, so drove down early this morning. Just pulled up not five minutes ago."

Which put him out of the running for murderer. *If* he really did arrive only five minutes ago. After all, he could have driven down last night, snuck up through the grounds, did the deed, and slipped away without anyone the wiser. We'd only his word.

"I'll still want to have a word with you," Cobblepot said. "After I've had a chat with the others. Lady Fortescue, the constable will take you to my office and get you a nice cup of tea."

It didn't escape either me or Freddy that he'd referred to it as "his" office. Apparently Cobblepot wasn't the sort to be cowed by Freddy's wealth or position.

"Come on down to the dining room, Alex," Freddy said. "I'll catch you up while Johnson whips up some whiskey and sodas."

"I could go for that," Alex said, clapping Freddy on the back. "Now, tell me, old man, what the deuce is going on around here?"

The police herded the rest of us along with them, although I wished they'd have left me alone. I needed time to think and maybe to poke around Lil's room for clues. Alas, it was not meant to be.

While Freddy rustled up drinks, the constable went around the room asking everyone whether or not their rooms had been messed with, and where they were between the times the rooms were searched by the police and Lady Fortescue had found hers awry. The answers were disappointingly the same. No one was missing anything, everyone's rooms were in perfect order, and all the guests had been in the dining room save for Malburn who'd just arrived.

Which meant that everyone except Malburn had a perfect alibi. Well, Malburn and the servants. They'd supposedly been in the kitchen, but had anyone been watching them? Perhaps among them we would find Raymond Frain's accomplice. For he must have one. It didn't make sense otherwise.

"Toni," I said, pulling her aside, "tell me about the first house party that was burgled."

"It was ever so exciting," she told me in a low voice. She took a sip of her whiskey and soda and continued. "It was at Lady Olivander's party. There must have been a dozen guests staying the week, plus another dozen that had been invited from the neighborhood. Dinner, dancing... you know the drill."

"Yes, of course," I said, though I'd no idea. The closest thing to a house party I'd ever been to was Christmas at my grandparents' with all the cousins. I doubted it was anything like Lady Olivander's party.

"Anyway, the locals had toddled off home, and we'd all gone to bed when there was this almighty crash. Everyone rushed out to find one of the statuaries toppled over and smashed on the floor."

"Oh, that's terrible," I said.

"It was," she agreed. "That statue was from ancient Rome. Can you imagine? It survives two thousand years only to be smashed to smithereens in Lady Olivander's foyer? The poor woman had a fit!" She took another slug of whiskey. "Anyway, once the hubbub had died down, we managed to get ourselves back to bed only to be roused again by a shriek. It was Lil. She claimed someone had been in her room, and a necklace was missing. Family heirloom or some such."

"Lil was the first to discover she'd been robbed?"

"Indeed, she was," Toni said. "That sent the rest of us scurrying to our rooms to see if anything had been taken."

"And had it?"

"But of course, darling. I was missing a ruby hatpin. Stupid little thing. More sentimental than valuable thought it looked costly. I never travel with my expensive jewelry you see. Let's see... Raymond was there, poor sod. He was missing a pocket watch. Probably the only thing of value he owned. Mary was missing a sapphire cocktail ring. Alex and Simon weren't there, so they got off scot-free. Sir Ruben—you haven't met him but he's a dear friend of Lady Olivander's—was missing a set of cuff links. And Vivian Moreton—ghastly woman—had a set of earrings and a bottle of perfume go missing."

"Perfume? That's an odd thing for a thief to take," I said. "What kind was it?"

"A Lanvin. Lovely stuff. No idea why anyone would steal it, though." She shrugged. "Maybe he's a pervert with a thing for fake blondes. Oh!" She slapped her hand over her mouth. "But the thief was Raymond, wasn't it? And one shouldn't speak ill of the dead."

I gave her a vague smile, unwilling to commit to Raymond's guilt one way or the other. "What about Freddy?"

"Oh, he wasn't there. He and Lady Olivander loathe each other."

Which confirmed what Jack had told me. "And the lady herself?"

"An antique gold bracelet, a scarab brooch, and some cash from the household cookie jar."

"It wasn't in her room?"

She shook her head. "The housekeeper reported it missing."

It seemed odd to me that one would entrust one's cash to a housekeeper, but then that was the wealthy for you. "So someone must have known the house well enough to know where the cash was kept."

"I suppose. I never really thought about it."

I was about to ask her about the rest of the thefts, when I realized Alex, the newcomer, had been left standing alone. This was my chance to speak to him! I strolled over to where he was holding up the wall, a tumbler of whiskey and soda in his hand. He eyed me over, raising one eyebrow in approval. Which was unusual. I wasn't unattractive, but men as handsome as Malburn rarely gave me a second glance.

I introduced myself. He did likewise, insisting I call him Alex.

"You're the American," he drawled. "How are you enjoying our little corner of the world? Such excitement."

"It was nice until somebody bumped off poor Mr. Frain."

"Yes, it's a shame about poor Ray. Nice enough chap." He took a swallow of whiskey. He didn't appear that upset. Perhaps they hadn't been close.

"You knew him well?"

"Not well, but well enough to know he didn't do what they're accusing him of." He swallowed another mouthful of booze and his eyes glittered bright and hard.

Interesting. "How can you be sure? It's surprising what people are capable of."

"Usually, yes, you are right. People are capable of the most astonishing things, but not Ray. Straight arrow. One of the good ones. And what'd he need with money, anyway?"

He made a good point, but was he just saying that because I was a stranger and that was what people her supposed to say? Or did he really mean it? I couldn't get a read on Alex. Total poker face.

I was about to ask another question when Lil marched into the room, sobbing wildly and dramatically. It had the immediate effect of the menfolk rushing to soothe her with sympathetic words and glasses of booze. Toni rolled her eyes, and Mary—who had been left by herself on the divan—let out a huff. Clearly neither woman was buying Lil's histrionics.

One by one, the police questioned the others, leaving Alex for last.

"He's scrummy, isn't he?" Toni said as Alex Malburn followed the constable from the room.

"I suppose." He was definitely good looking.

"Too bad he's poor as a church mouse."

"Really? I thought he was supposed to be fabulously wealthy."

She gave me a sly look. "Oh, he will be. When his uncle kicks off. But until then, he's on a very tight leash. Mustn't upset dear Uncle."

I eyed the empty doorway where he'd passed through. How interesting. That meant that Alexander Malburn probably needed money. Or wanted it, at any rate. Could he have been Raymond's partner and therefore his killer?

Somehow or other I needed to check his alibi. Had he really been on the road from London? Or had he been sneaking in to murder poor Raymond Frain?

A yawn overtook me and so, with permission of the constable, I took myself off to bed. Maybe things would make more sense much later in the morning.

Later that day, I made my way down to breakfast. It was around ten and Penny had already collected Tippy for his own breakfast and walk.

When I thanked her, she waved it off. "I've got extra time, Miss."

"Oh? Why's that?"

"Simon—Mr. Parlance—doesn't want me cleaning his room. Keeps it locked and everything. Which means more time for this little guy." She'd scrubbed Tippy's head and his little nub of a tail wagged furiously as she led him from the room.

I thought it was strange that Simon didn't want his room cleaned, but then people were particular about things like that. Maybe he just didn't want her seeing his under things or was afraid she'd break something.

I was the only one at the table and helped myself to toast, strawberry jam, and coffee, ignoring the sausages, kippers, and other heavy foods. I honestly wasn't used to eating much more than toast to start my day and was already feeling bloated from the rich food and overindulgence.

"Message for you, Miss," Johnson said, appearing by my side like a wraith.

"You nearly gave me a heart attack!" I clutched my chest.

"Apologies." He didn't sound at all apologetic as he laid an envelope next to my plate and strode away.

The missive was from Jack. He wanted to meet in the Sullen Oyster at eleven. I glanced at my wristwatch. It was ten fifteen now. If I hurried, I could get dressed, collect Tippy, and head down to the village.

I didn't examine why I was so eager to see him, assuring myself it was simply professional. I just wanted to hear what he'd found out. That was it.

And I might have a bridge in Arizona to sell you.

Cramming toast in my mouth and downing the last swallow of coffee, I dashed up the stairs to my room. I figured my simple blue A-line skirt and white blouse were fine, so I threw my new pink raincoat over the top and grabbed my handbag. Good enough.

Tippy was not best pleased to be dragged out for another walk. Especially as the gray gloom had turned into a veritable downpour. But I couldn't leave him alone in the house, despite what he might wish, and I could use a guard dog. Not that a creature with two-inch-long legs was much protection, but strangely, he made me feel better.

I was kind of having fun, tromping along in what Johnson had called "Wellies." Rain boots to the rest of us. Perhaps it was a bit childlike, stomping in puddles, but it was a nice stress reliever, let me tell you.

All the way down the hill, I pondered last night's events. Or rather this morning's events. Poor Raymond. Maybe he was the thief, but he certainly hadn't deserved to die. But how interesting that he'd been killed in exactly the same way Lil had threatened on doing it. To my mind, that meant that either Lil had done exactly what she'd said she'd do—which would be incredibly stupid of her—or the killer had been in the room—or near enough to it—to overhear her threat and figured it was as good a way as any to get rid of poor Raymond while pinning it on someone else.

Either way, it didn't really clarify things. We'd all be in the room except for the servants and Alexander Malburn. Not that any of that meant anything. Any of the servants could have been hovering in the hall. I read enough books to know that happens. As for Malburn, well, until the police confirmed his alibi, I had to consider that he could have driven down a day early and snuck around.

And then there was the fact that anyone who did hear Lil's threat could have told someone else about it. Who and why was anyone's guess, but it was a distinct possibility. Which meant that anyone in the house, and quite a few people outside of it, could be the killer.

So not only had I not solved the robbery, exactly, I now had a murder on my hands.

"I hear you found the thief," Jack said without preamble when I took my seat in the corner booth at the Sullen Oyster. Tippy glared at me from outside the window, despite the fact he was under the overhang and not getting rained on at all.

"What do you mean?"

He passed me a half pint of ale. I had no idea why. It wasn't even noon. But I supposed if we were going to take up a booth, we should buy something. What I could really use was more coffee, though I doubt I could find it in this place.

"It's all over the village. Raymond Frain was murdered last night, and they found jewelry on him which he'd stolen from one of the guests. It would appear the thief was caught."

"So it would appear," I said dryly, twisting the glass in my hands. I didn't take a drink. I loathe beer of any kind. And this kind in particular was malodorous. I didn't know how he could drink it and at eleven in the morning. "Except that your gossip is wrong. The police didn't find anything on him."

It was his turn to look confused. "Are you saying Frain wasn't the thief?"

"I'm saying it's awfully convenient that the very night after a guest threatens to bash the thief over the head with a poker, Raymond Frain turns up dead, bashed over the head with a poker." I gave him a quick rundown on what had happened.

He sat back. "Bloody hell."

"You got that right."

"Do you think he was guilty? Frain?"

"Well," I twisted the glass some more, "he was at all five of the parties that were robbed, according to you."

"That's right. My uncle confirmed it."

"And he was one of only three guests who were. The others being Mary Parlance and Toni."

"Toni is it?"

I shrugged. "I like her. She's given me lots of information on the other guests, both those at Lord Chasterly's and those not."

He lifted a brow. "That still doesn't mean she's not involved."

"No, it doesn't," I admitted reluctantly. I hated to think of Toni as the bad guy. She was so charming, but I knew very well that charming people could do bad things. Before I met Sam, I'd once gone on a date with a very charming man. He'd stuck me with the bill. "Listen, I need you to find out for me Alexander Malburn's location the last couple of days."

"Seriously?"

"Yes, seriously. The man arrived right after we discovered a dead body on the premises. If that isn't suspicious, I don't know what is."

He ran a hand through his hair. "That doesn't mean anything. Maybe he's telling the truth, and he just drove down this morning."

"And maybe he's lying," I countered.

"How am I supposed to find out when he left London?"

"I don't know. Talk to his neighbors or something," I said. "Surely they'd notice when he left. His car was in the drive. It's a bright red Roadster. Not exactly quiet. If he really left London early this morning, they'd have heard it."

"Fine," he grumbled. "I'll head back today and see what I can find out. Meet me here tomorrow morning."

I glanced around. "I'd rather not. How about the cafe just down the street? It looks really nice. And there's a sign that says they serve fresh scones. I've never had a scone."

He huffed. "Fine. Tomorrow. Ten."

"I'll see you then. One more thing."

"Yes?"

I winced. "The brooch you gave me is missing."

"I thought you said nothing was found on Frain."

"It wasn't. Which means if he was the thief, he's got an accomplice, and if he wasn't..."

"He's being framed," Jack said.

"You're being very calm about this," I said nervously. "Why aren't you more upset about your brooch?"

"Because I have every confidence you'll find it when you find the killer."

I swallowed. "But what if I don't?"

He gave me a look rife with meaning. "Then you'll have to make it up to me."

I don't know why, but I blushed scarlet and scurried out of the pub, away from prying eyes—and Jack—as quickly as I could. I rescued Tippy who was still giving me the cold shoulder for leaving him in the rain.

I probably should have given Jack a piece of my mind for being so...shameless. On the other hand, just thinking about it made me giddy. However, I had a job to do and didn't have time to moon over handsome men.

I had a full day before I could discover if Alex was telling the truth about his alibi. In the meantime, I needed to find out everything I could about the other parties and guests and what had been stolen.

I mulled over the facts as Tippy and I wandered slowly back to Endmere, ignoring the rain drizzling around us. The facts as I saw them were these:

1. There had been five house parties in Devon which had been robbed.

2. Of all the guests invited to these parties, only ten—if one included Lord Chasterly—had been at more than one of the house parties.

3. Of all the guests at the various parties, only three had been to all five parties. And of those three, one of them was dead.

I shuddered. Somehow that seemed a bad omen.

Chapter 10

I arrived back at the manor, dripping wet, to find the house in an uproar. Shouting echoed down the hall. Something crashed like glass splintering against stone. A woman shrieked angrily.

Penny was just crossing the foyer as I entered. "Goodness, Miss, you're all wet. Here." She thrust a fancy linen hanky on me.

"Oh, but this is too nice?" I said, noticing a small tear amongst the curlicued embroidery.

"Pish posh. Better than dripping all over the floor. Lord Chasterly has a whole stack of them. A woman from the village makes them for him. Just give it back when you're done, and I'll get it mended then and back to him. He'll never notice it's missing."

"Thanks, Penny. You're a doll."

As I handed Tippy off to Penny, I asked, "What on Earth happened?"

"Young Mr. Simon accused Lady Fortescue of killing poor Mr. Frain," she whispered. "Said she done him in just like she said she would."

"Oh, dear," I murmured.

"You got that right. Lady Fortescue, well, I don't like to speak ill of my betters, but she lost the plot a bit, if you know what I mean."

"I assume that means she had a temper tantrum."

"Rather! Started screaming and throwing things and—when his lordship told her to stop at once—she started bawling her eyes out." Penny's own eyes were wide with excitement. "Lady Netherford—"

"Wait, that's Toni, right?" I was starting to lose track what with all the Lord this and my Lady that. I was glad I was a plain Miss.

"Yes, Miss. Lady Netherford told Lady Fortescue to cut the dramatics, and Lady Fortescue tried to strangle her."

"Holy cow," I muttered.

"Indeed, Miss. Mr. Malburn tried to break it up, and Lady Fortescue slapped him and accused *him* of killing Mr. Frain. Which is nonsense, of course. How could someone as handsome as Mr. Malburn be a murderer?"

Which was the most ridiculous case for innocence I'd ever heard. William Heirens, known as the Lipstick Killer, had been caught just two years ago. He'd confessed to killing three people. I'd seen his picture in the paper and though he wasn't my type, plenty of girls had thought he was good looking. Didn't make him any less guilty.

At just that moment, Mary Parlance descended the stairs. She had an oddly majestic way about her like she just expected every head to turn and every eye to be on her. In this case, they certainly were, even though the only eyes present were mine, Penny's, and Tippy's. And Tippy wasn't impressed. I was, though. Mary was the sort of girl that just glowed golden: golden hair, golden skin, and gold-flecked blue eyes. No doubt she'd been born with a gold spoon in her mouth rather than a silver one. Her slender figure looked well in a gray belted dress.

"Quite a ruckus," she said in an unperturbed tone.

Penny opened her mouth, probably to give Mary the same story she'd given me, but Mary walked past her like she wasn't even there. I half expected Penny to be upset, but she didn't even blink. Like this was business as usual. And maybe it was. These fancy people sure liked to treat their staff like they were so much wallpaper.

"Come on, Tippy," Penny said. "Let's go downstairs and find you a treat."

Tippy's tail wagged wildly as he followed her to the kitchen. He knew what "treat" meant. He was incredibly smart when he wanted to be. The rest of the time I swear he had selective hearing.

I followed Mary into the sitting room which the police had finally released. We were about to enter when Lil came storming out, face red and blotchy, eyes burning with inner fire and ringed in running mascara.

"I'm not staying here another minute," she shouted as she marched up the stairs.

"The police won't be happy," I murmured. "They seemed very serious about everyone staying put."

"Oh, but she's *Lady* Fortescue," Mary said, as if that explained everything. Which maybe it did. England wasn't the only place where wealth and status could get a person out of a sticky situation.

Problem was, how was I expected to do my job if all the suspects flew the coop? I dithered. Perhaps if I approached it just right...

"Will you excuse me?" I said to Mary. "I need to visit the ladies' room."

She gave me a blank look. "Do what you want. I don't care."

I hurried up the stairs and down the hall to Lil's room. The door stood wide open, and an open suitcase lay on the bed. She was in a fury, throwing things in willy-nilly without even waiting for a maid. Admittedly, I wouldn't have waited for a maid, but I'm not used to having one and Lil was. Or at least, I assumed so based on what I knew of English society.

I rapped on the door and waited for her to look up.

"Oh, it's you." She went back to throwing things in her case. By now it was completely overflowing, and a slinky rose-pink silk dress slipped to puddle on the floor.

I stepped in and picked it up, laying it carefully across the bed. "I just thought I'd check on you. You've had such a fright."

That stopped her. She stared at me, a Copen blue peignoir clutched to her chest. "What do you mean?"

"Well," I said thoughtfully, "your jewelry getting stolen. Then the police accusing you of horrible things. It must have been terrible."

She almost wilted. "You see! You understand. It *is* terrible, and I didn't do it. Truly I didn't."

"Of course not. Anyone can see that." I didn't offer any reason as to why since the truth was, anyone *couldn't* see that. She was shaping up to be the perfect suspect even in my eyes, but pointing that out wouldn't do me any favors if I wanted to get information out of her. "And this isn't the first time. You poor thing. I can't imagine having to deal with so many robberies. What a trial."

She sank down on the bed. "You are so right. It's been exhausting constantly worrying about my things getting stolen or being murdered in my bed. And then the police and everyone accusing me of killing Raymond. As if

I ever would. Not that he didn't deserve it. Ghastly business. How dare he steal from his betters!"

"Uh, sorry, I thought Mr. Frain was one of your circle?" At least that was the feeling I got from everyone else.

She snorted. "Hardly. Young upstart. Son of nobody. He just got lucky, and people like his trashy novels."

Sounded like bitter grapes to me. Here she was, a woman of title and position but no money, probably because she thought working was beneath her. Meanwhile, Raymond Frain worked his backside off and made good, but because he didn't have a title, she thought she was better than he was. I disliked her more all the time, but that didn't mean she was a murderer. Didn't mean she wasn't, either.

"Where are you going to go?" I asked, taking out a slip and folding it neatly. My mother had taught me to fold clothes from the tender age of five. I'd never been very particular about it, but I could do a half decent job of it.

"Home, of course," she said. "I'm tired of the country. At least there are things to do in London." Although she looked a little pinched around the eyes as if she was worried. I was betting London was difficult when one was broke.

I folded a sweater and then a blouse. "That makes sense. London is so exciting. I'd never been abroad before until I arrived in London."

She sniffed a little haughtily I thought. "Let the maid do that."

"I thought you were in a hurry."

"I am, but it should be done right." She got up and grabbed a train case from the top of the wardrobe. With one sweep of her hand, she shoved everything off the vanity into it.

I winced at the sound of something breaking. The strong aroma of roses filled the air, and I sneezed.

Lil let out a very unladylike word. "I guess I'll have to visit Harrods and get that replaced."

I wondered if she could afford it or if she planned to steal it. That thought shocked me. When had I become such a suspicious person? Possibly the day Mr. Woodward had hired me to poke my nose into strangers' business. "I thought the police wanted everyone to stay here."

"The police can hang," she snapped. "I didn't have anything to do with this, and they can't make me stay."

I was pretty sure she was wrong about that. "Maybe we can prove to them you had an alibi." Not to mention it would allow me to find out what her alibi was, if she had one.

She blinked at me. "An alibi?"

"Yes. For the time of Mr. Frain's murder. If we show them you couldn't possibly have done it, then they have to let you go back to London, don't they?"

"I suppose you're right. How do we do that?"

"Well," I pretended to mull it over. "First, I suppose we need to establish a timeline."

"All right." She set her train case on the vanity and sank onto the stool.

"For instance, what time did you go to bed last night?"

"Early," she said. "You were there, and you saw me leave."

"That's right." She'd claimed to have a headache. "That was about ten. I went up right after you."

"So you're my alibi?"

"Afraid not. Everyone else, including Frain, was still awake and in the sitting room. I fell asleep almost right away, so I'm no use."

"Oh."

"According to the police, Frain was killed between midnight and two in the morning," I said. "Where were you then?"

"Asleep, of course. I took headache powders and went straight to bed."

"But you woke up, right?"

"Yes." She tapped her chin with a peach-colored nail. "I woke about a quarter to three. I was feeling a bit muzzy-headed and thirsty, so I went into the lavatory to get some water. Then I went back to bed, but I couldn't fall asleep again."

"So you got up?"

"Yes. I thought maybe some fresh air. A walk in the garden," she said. "Then I heard the scream like everyone else, and I ran downstairs."

And then there was Raymond's poor dead body and the rest of us gathered around it.

She sighed heavily. "It's not a very good alibi, is it?"

"Afraid not."

She shook her head. "I never did have any luck unless it was rotten."

Until I heard back from Jack about Alexander Malburn's whereabouts the night of the murder, there wasn't anything I could do about him. Next on the list would have to be the Parlances.

According to Toni, Simon hadn't been at the first house party, which likely meant he wasn't a viable suspect, but it didn't rule him out entirely. I wanted to know why he hadn't gone, and his sister had, since the two of them seemed inseparable by all accounts.

I caught Simon in the library, reading a book. I don't know why that surprised me. I suppose I'd assumed that with his tanned skin and fit physique, he was one of those sporty types who hadn't time for cerebral pursuits.

"Oh, sorry," I said cheerfully. "I didn't realize anyone was in here." Which was an utter lie, of course, though I was getting pretty good at it. Lying, I mean. I wondered if I should worry about that.

He glanced up, his expression warming when he saw me. "No worries." He set the book aside. It was a collection of Shakespeare's sonnets. Double surprise. "Can I be of assistance? What are you looking for?"

My mind went blank. "Oh, just something light to read. Trying to take my mind off all this." I waved my hand in the general direction of the sitting room.

"It is quite shocking," he said sympathetically.

"Very. I've never been involved in a criminal investigation before."

He smiled. "It's not terribly exciting. Especially as the police like to keep you cooped up in the house until they're satisfied you didn't do it."

"You make it sound like you've been through this before." I perched on the chair across from him and studied his face. Good heavens to Betsy, he was handsome.

"I have. This is my fourth time, actually."

"Fourth!" I let out a dramatic gasp.

"Well, the other three weren't murders." He chuckled, but it sounded forced.

"You mean those robberies Toni told me about," I said, throwing poor Lady Netherfield under the bus.

He chuckled again, but his eyes weren't smiling. "That woman does love to gab. Yes, that's what I mean. Each time I've been stuck at some loathsome country house longer than I wished."

"Why do you go to them if you don't like them? The country house parties, I mean."

He didn't answer, only gave me a somewhat sly look. Which only increased my suspicions.

"You said four, but weren't there five robberies?" I asked instead.

"Ah, yes, of course, but I wasn't at the first. My sister was. Believe me, I heard all about it."

"Weren't you invited?" I clapped my hand over my mouth as if suddenly realizing I was being gauche. Sometimes it paid off if people thought you were a bumbling idiot. "Oh, sorry. That was rude, wasn't it?"

He laughed. "I was invited, of course. Mary and I usually go everywhere together, but I was a bit under the weather that week, so I stayed home. In London. Poor Mary. She's said she'll never go to another party unless I'm there."

Yet another thing I'd need Jack to check on. I'd have to use Freddy's phone and ring up Mr. Woodward's office. Surely he could get Jack a message.

"I don't blame her," I said. "It would have been terribly nerve wracking to be alone at such a horrible time."

"You're alone, and you seemed to manage."

"Ah, well, it probably has to do with my work during the war."

He raised a brow. "Were you a spy or something? How exciting."

I burst out laughing. "No. I worked in the shipyards. As a welder."

"How... interesting." He didn't sound interested. He sounded appalled.

"We all had to do our bit," I reminded him.

"True. But welding. It's such a masculine occupation, isn't it?"

"I'm certain you had women welders here," I said a little defensively.

"Of course. But not of *our* class of person."

Oh, right, because I was supposed to be wealthy. I decided a swift subject change was called for. "What would you be doing if you weren't stuck here?"

He launched into a long and boring soliloquy about his love for fast cars and his plans for some race or other. I admit I tuned him out, giving a vague smile and nod where appropriate. It did the trick. He kept blathering, completely unaware that he would have been boring me to tears if I'd been paying attention.

Based on his clothing and his talking of race cars, it didn't seem like he needed money, but that didn't mean anything. He could have done the burglaries out of sheer boredom. Nor did missing out on the first party rule him out. Devon wasn't that far from London by car, and if he was a racing driver, he could have easily made it out here, robbed the party, and gone back in record time.

He may not be top of my list, but Simon was still very definitely in my crosshairs. At least for now.

"And Mary goes with you to these races?" I asked when he stopped for air.

"Oh, no. She doesn't care for them. Says they're loud and smelly and there are no interesting men." He guffawed at that.

So they weren't as joined at the hip as everyone thought. Which made it odd that they always went to house parties together. Oh, sure, there was the excuse that she was scared about the robberies, but she hadn't seemed scared to me. She'd seemed... annoyed and maybe a little angry.

I was definitely going to have to dive deeper into this brother and sister duo. But for now, I didn't trust them. Not one bit.

Chapter 11

The morning rain had stopped and the gloom had burned off, leaving the countryside around the manor house drenched in dappled sunlight. Light sparkled off the waves crashing beneath the cliff, and little white sails bobbed out at sea. I wasn't sure if they were fishing boats or pleasure craft. Didn't matter. It was terribly picturesque.

After leaving a message for Jack with Mr. Woodward, I wandered outside to enjoy the sunshine. Steam curled off dripping greenery and the air hung heavy and moist, smelling of petrichor and sea salt.

I found Mary sunning herself in the garden. Which seemed a little strange to me. A man had just been murdered. A man who, if not her friend, had certainly been an acquaintance. A member of her circle. Now here she was not twelve hours later lounging on a lawn chair in nothing but a hot pink bikini and a pair of the new harlequin-style sunglasses in green plastic frames.

I'd never seen a real live person wearing a bikini before. Naturally, I'd seen the photos when the garment had first come out two years previously. Such scandal had ensued! All that bared flesh. Shocking!

Personally, I thought they were rather nice if one had the figure for it. And clearly Mary had. Plus all that gorgeous bronzed skin. I was a little envious of her bravery and her tan.

"What a lovely day," I said inanely.

"I suppose," she drawled, not moving.

I took a lawn chair in the shade. I am woefully pale and tend to turn red as a lobster in the sun, which also gives me a headache if the light is too bright. I wondered if I could get a pair of harlequin sunglasses like Mary's. In blue, maybe. Blue is my favorite color.

The patio was a lovely warm golden stone with a low balustrade around it, no doubt to keep tipsy guests from falling off into the shrubbery. A small pond sat off to the right, little golden fish flitting back and forth and fresh blooming peonies dipping their fluffy pink heads in the slight breeze.

"Did you want something?" she asked rudely.

"I was just talking to your brother."

"Oh?" She sounded bored.

"He was telling me about the first house party robbery."

She sniffed but remained otherwise relaxed and unaffected. "What would he know about it? He wasn't there."

"He told me what you went through," I pressed on, hoping to get something out of her. "Must have been terrifying."

"I guess." She tilted her chin as if to catch more sun, but I'd a feeling she was peeping at me from beneath her glasses.

I kept my gaze on the pond as if there were nothing more fascinating in the world to me than the fish. "I can't even imagine it. I wouldn't have slept a wink."

"Who says I did?" This time her tone was coated with amusement.

"You're so brave."

She turned her head, lifted her glasses, and stared at me. "Why do you say that?"

"Well, you kept going. To the parties, I mean. Even with all those terrible robberies. I think I'd have given up and stayed home with my doors locked."

"Oh, well, I had Simon with me after the first one, so it wasn't so bad." She dropped her glasses back into place.

"Yes. Simon told me he was sick and had to miss it."

She laughed as if whatever I'd said was hysterically funny. "Of course."

"You mean he wasn't sick?" I said, feigning surprise. It was no shock to me I'd been lied to. Simon had struck me as the sort who liked to color the truth to suit his purpose.

"That's what we *told* everyone, but the truth was he was having a torrid affair with a married woman, and her husband was gone that weekend. He didn't want to upset Lady Olivander—she's terribly sweet—so we pretended he was sick."

"Oh, I see," I said, trying not to sound judgmental. I did not approve of philandering. Nor did I approve of lying to one's hostess about being ill. I wasn't here to judge, but to solve a crime. If Simon hadn't been ill, he could have been involved in the robbery. Unless, of course, the married woman could give him an alibi. "Are they still seeing each other?"

"Who?"

"Simon and the married woman? Is it anyone I know?"

"I doubt it, and no, they broke it off ages ago."

I'd hoped she'd give me a name, but apparently she either wasn't interested in juicy gossip or that easily manipulated. Still, maybe Jack would be able to dig it up.

"Anyway, now he's dead. Raymond, I mean. So there won't be any more robberies, will there?" she said.

"I suppose not," I agreed, a little shocked at her callous tone. She seemed completely unperturbed the poor man had been brutally killed mere hours before. "Aren't you upset?"

"Well, he wasn't *our* sort of person, was he?"

That was the second time someone had said that to me in as many days. As if having not been born into wealth and power, Frain somehow deserved his death. Or, at the very least, his death was inconsequential. Never mind that he had achieved success on his own without it being spoon-fed to him, or that he'd been a kind person, at least to me in the brief time I'd known him. I still couldn't wrap my head around him being the thief. It just didn't sit right.

But I said none of this. I wasn't sure I could trust Mary, so I made my excuses and went up to my room.

Could Mary have been involved?

According to Toni, Simon and Mary had plenty of money, which meant they didn't need to go around stealing things. But people stole for reasons other than necessity.

Growing up, we'd had a neighbor, Mrs. Dudley. She was a dear woman. Very kind. Always bringing us fresh baked coffee cakes and jam made from blackberries she picked herself. Unfortunately, every time she visited some little trinket would go missing. Fortunately, her long-suffering husband would appear on our doorstep later that day with the same item clutched in his sweaty hand and stammering apologies. I later read about kleptomania at the library. Fascinating stuff. I'd felt very sorry for poor Mrs. Dudley.

I doubted the thief—or thieves—in this case were kleptomaniacs. Mrs. Dudley had never taken anything valuable. She'd usually stuck to small things like thimbles or a lipstick. Often we wouldn't even realize they'd gone missing until Mr. Dudley returned them.

That was totally unlike the items stolen from the house parties. Those must have all together been worth thousands of pounds. Which, to my mind, indicated that this was neither the work of a kleptomaniac, nor someone who was simply bored and wanted to see if they could get away with it. No, the thief was in it for the money, of that I had no doubt. Which meant that someone at this house party was lying about their financial status.

Based on the list of robbery victims, I couldn't really narrow it down. While not all guests had been robbed at all the parties, everyone had at least one item stolen. Which was smart. That way the actual thief didn't stand out.

Lil was the only person I could absolutely guarantee hadn't been lying about her income.

She was broke. Everyone had said so, and she had even admitted it. For her, the robberies had been devastating both financially and emotionally.

A woman of her status would never lie about being broke. I mean, they would lie and say they *weren't* broke, but they wouldn't admit they had no money and were basically using the house parties to keep a roof over their heads and food in their bellies. So while that gave her an excellent motive to commit the robberies, the very fact she *had* admitted it and that it was known amongst her set meant she likely wasn't involved. It would have put too big of a mark on her.

No, the thief or thieves had to be keeping up appearances. Poor, but not admitting it. Desperately holding on to their image by a thread, terrified that someone might find out. Which meant it could be any one of the others. It also meant that it was someone willing to steal and murder their own friends to keep their secret. And that made them extremely dangerous.

Jack met me at the cafe as planned. It was a cute little place with a thatched roof and a forest green door. There were half a dozen tables covered in green and white polka-dot cloths and set for two. The wooden chairs were painted white to match. A long counter displayed glass-covered plates of fluffy looking scones and rich layer cakes.

Over leek soup and cheese sandwiches—a nice change from the lavish meals up at Endmere—he told me what he'd found out about the alibis.

"Alexander Malburn's alibi holds true. He was with a few mates at a drinking establishment in London until gone midnight. According to them, he went home earlier than usual claiming he had to drive to Devon early in the morning."

I frowned, mulling it over. "He could have driven straight from the club here and made it in time to kill Raymond."

"True. Except that I also spoke with his neighbor, a Mrs. Merriton. She's..." He hesitated. "She's quite up on the goings on in the neighborhood."

I laughed. "You mean she's nosey. Like Mrs. Dudley back home."

He raised a brow. "Mrs. Dudley?"

"Sure. Growing up, Mr. and Mrs. Dudley were an elderly couple who lived across the street. Any time one of us kids stepped a foot wrong, Mrs. Dudley was over at our place telling Mama all about it. The time a neighbor kid stole a pear off our tree, Mrs. Dudley was over in a flash. Someone new moved to the neighborhood, Mrs. Dudley knew who they were, where they'd come from, and why they'd moved in all within an hour or two."

"Good lord. She'd give MI6 a run for their money."

"No doubt." Except for the petty theft part, but I didn't mention that.

"Well, Mrs. Merriton appears to be the exact same sort of woman. She assured me that not only did Mr. Malburn arrive home around half past twelve—she doesn't sleep well, apparently—but that he left at the ungodly hour of six in the morning."

"That would jive with his arrival time." I sighed. "I guess he's out. There's no way he could have killed Raymond Frain."

"Doesn't let him off the hook for the robberies though, does it?"

"No, it doesn't. Although it would definitely mean he had an accomplice." I bit the nail of my right thumb then reminded myself ladies don't bite their nails. "What about Simon Parlance? He told me he was ill during the first party which was why he missed it. However, his sister claimed he was actually with a married woman. What's the truth?"

He smiled grimly. "Apparently, it is a not-very-well-held secret that Simon Parlance was having an affair with Abigail Bently, the wife of Sir John Bently. I spoke with her and Simon was, indeed, with her during the party. They've since split up, and she's not happy about it, so she told me something else."

"What?" I leaned forward eagerly.

"They were not in London. Simon had rented a small seaside cottage about a twenty-minute drive from the manor house where the first party took place. She claims to have woken in the middle of the night to find him gone. He did not return until right before dawn. When she asked where he'd gone, he told her he couldn't sleep so had gone out for a drive."

"That's rather suspicious."

"It gets better. When news came out about the robbery, she thought nothing of it until he told her that if anyone asked, she was to say they were in London together."

My jaw dropped. "Did he really?"

"Indeed he did. She was immediately suspicious, but he claimed it was because he had no alibi and was afraid the police might accuse him wrongfully."

"She no doubt brushed it off, not wanting to think of her lover as a criminal," I mused.

He nodded. "Yes, that is what I assumed as well. She confirmed it."

I mulled it over. "So he has no alibi at all. In fact, he was within easy drive of the crime. He could very well be the thief as well as the murderer."

"I have something else for you." Jack handed me a piece of folded paper.

I unfolded it eagerly. There were three handwritten columns. The first held a list of items—the stolen ones, I assumed. The second, a list of names, each one lining up with one of the items. And the third were what looked like the names of the manor houses from which the items were stolen, numbered one through five.

"This is brilliant!" I said. "And none of these items has turned up in pawn shops or anything?"

"Not that the police have found."

"And the thief would have had no time to sell the ones from the most recent burglary." An idea was taking shape. "I need to search the house."

Shéa MacLeod

Chapter 12

After collecting Tippy, I charged back up the hill to the manor house. He was not happy about it and dragged his feet, giving me the evil eye every time I turned around to scold him.

I knew that Lil's bracelet had been stolen, but I hadn't yet heard if anything else had been taken other than my—Jack's—brooch. I hadn't managed to escape the thief's clutches even though I'd had Tippy in my room. Either the thief had watched me closely, knowing when Tippy was there and wasn't, or he'd taken a chance and gotten lucky.

By the time the manor came into view, I was puffing and panting. I handed Tippy off to Johnson who promised to pass him along to Penny. He gave me one last glare as they departed—Tippy, not Johnson. Johnson barely looked at me.

The list hadn't had Lil's bracelet on it, of course, nor any mention of Endmere. It had only had the first four robberies. There was one person who would be able to tell me what had been stolen. I went in search of Lord Chasterly.

The sitting room was empty, as was the dining room and library. I found Toni on the back patio, drinking a blue cocktail out of a martini glass.

"Oh, Sugar, why don't you join me!" she called from behind her big, bug-eyed sunglasses. "Johnson makes the most marvelous Blue Moon. It tastes like heaven!"

It did sound tasty, but I had work to do. "Sorry, Toni. Maybe later. Right now, I need to speak to Freddy."

"Oh, he's gone off with Simon hunting or fishing or something."

Tarnation. I may have even said that aloud.

She slid her glasses down her nose and peered at me over the white plastic frames. "That's an interesting word. What does it mean?"

Yep, I sure did say it aloud. "Erm, nothing important. Where's everyone else?"

"Lil is taking a nap in her room, and Alex and Mary went to the village. Why?"

"Listen," I sat down at the table next to her, "do you know if anything else was stolen the night Frain was killed? Besides Lil's bracelet, I mean." I didn't mention my—I mean Jack's—brooch.

She tapped a coral colored nail against the table. "I do believe Mary had a ring go missing. An opal dress ring with yellow diamonds. Worth a few bob. She was furious about it."

"I'm surprised she didn't mention it."

"She told the police of course," Toni said, taking a sip of her drink. "But she didn't want anyone else to know. I only do because I overheard her telling her brother. Or rather, screaming at her brother."

It seemed strange she wouldn't want anyone to know and then scream about it, but then Mary did come off as a bit arrogant. Maybe she saw losing the ring as a weakness or something. Or maybe yelling about it was her passive aggressive way of letting everyone know without actually admitting anything was wrong. "Anything else?"

"Freddy said a Dresden figurine that belonged to his mother was missing from the mantle in the morning room. He never uses the room, so I'm surprised he noticed it was gone."

"The police did tell us all to look around," I pointed out.

"True. Maybe that's it."

It was interesting, though. Why would he think to look for missing items in a room that was never used? Perhaps he was just paranoid. After five robberies, he had the right to be. I was beginning to think I was as bad at this undercover business as I was at being a secretary.

"What about you?" I asked. "Were you missing anything?"

"Not a thing," she said cheerfully. "In fact, no one else was. Alex, because he wasn't here. Frain, because he was the thief. And I'm assuming Simon and I lucked out because Lil caught Frain and coshed him upside the head."

"You seem sure Lil is guilty."

"Isn't she?" Toni said placidly. "I admit, I don't like the woman much, but she did threaten to kill the thief in exactly the manner poor Raymond was killed."

"Yes, well, I'm not so sure. And I'm not sure Raymond was the thief." I rose and started for the house.

"Where are you going?" she called after me.

"Just thought I'd explore a bit. Haven't had a chance to," I said.

"How dull. Well, I'll be out here with drinkies if you need me."

I took the stairs to the second floor—or what everyone else called the first floor—and hesitated on the landing, unsure where to start. I knew what I was looking for: an opal ring and a Dresden figurine, as well as my brooch and Lil's bracelet. Problem was I wasn't sure *where* to look.

The obvious answer was everyone's rooms. Frain hadn't had any of the items on him, so I was betting the real thief had taken them. No doubt they were far too valuable to be left behind. Otherwise it would have been an excellent opportunity to make sure the frame stuck. Although, everyone seemed happy to consider Frain the thief anyway.

But would the thief really keep stolen items in his or her room? It was hard to say. I supposed it depended on their psychology. Whether they were the sort to want to keep the objects close where they could keep an eye on them, or far away in case they were found.

Since Lil was in her room, I couldn't search there. The whole frame job was an obvious red herring. Of course, it *could* be the sort of red herring to make me think she was innocent when she really was guilty, but I doubted it. Yes, she had the motive, being impoverished and angry about losing precious heirlooms, but she seemed far more focused on snaring a man to solve her problems rather than solving them on her own.

Uncertain when everyone would be back, I decided to search Simon's room first as, to my mind, he was the most likely suspect. After all, he had no alibi for the first robbery.

What I found was a man who clearly had no respect for his possessions. Clothing and accessories were strewn willy-nilly around, and the room reeked of cologne as if a bottle had been overturned. A pile of dirty towels sat in the chair, and the waste bin was overflowing. I remembered Penny telling me Simon hadn't wanted the maids in his room. Interesting. Could it be because he was hiding something nefarious?

What I did not find was any sign that Simon was the thief. There wasn't a single trace of any of the stolen items, nor was there anything suspicious like a balaclava or a set of lock picks. Although he wouldn't need lock picks, of course, having been invited in. And while there were gloves, they were fingerless lambskin driving gloves, so it wasn't like those would have done him any good in the breaking and stealing department. It seemed that my suspicions were unfounded.

Frain's room was next. He was dead, of course, but maybe there was some clue there.

Unlike Simon, Raymond Frain had brought few possessions. The wardrobe contained a tweed jacket—far too heavy for this time of year—a pair of neatly pressed trousers, and two white button-down shirts. A pair of brushes and some hair oil sat on top of the dresser which contained his incidentals. Next to the bed was a fountain pen and a notebook filled with scribbled notes, perhaps ideas for his next book. Inside the single drawer of the nightstand was a bottle of pills for blood pressure. Next to that was his wallet and bank book.

Curiosity hit me and I scooped up the book. It contained all Raymond's deposits and withdrawals into his accounts. And, if these were correct, so much for Freddy's claims that Raymond was broke. Far from being destitute, our struggling writer had five thousand pounds in the bank! Why would Freddy lie about something like that? Perhaps he didn't know. After all, the English thought money talk was crass, so perhaps Freddy was assuming things based on outward appearances. After all, Raymond certainly didn't dress like a man with a wad of cash.

Onward. Both Toni's and Mary's rooms revealed nothing, although that wasn't much of a surprise. Both were overly fond of cosmetics, although Toni was also clearly obsessed with face creams. Perhaps because she was older. I understood her concern. Both had wardrobes crammed full of expensive fashions. Both had surprisingly lurid romances on their bedside tables. And neither had stolen valuables hidden anywhere. Although I noticed that Mary's held a round Lanvin perfume bottle. The same kind of perfume that had been stolen during the first robbery. It was odd, but probably a coincidence.

Alex's room was next, though I'd little hope of uncovering anything. After all, Jack had confirmed his alibi. He could neither be the killer, nor the thief. I supposed, however, he could be an accomplice.

The room was tidy and smelled of bay rum. Rather pleasant, I thought. A search of his wardrobe and drawers revealed that while he had excellent taste, he wasn't our thief, although there was a nice wad of cash tucked away in a sock. Toni had said he hadn't much money, at least until his uncle died. Was she wrong? Lying? I hoped not. I was about to leave the room when I noticed a pair of his shoes tucked under the edge of the bed.

I couldn't have said what drew me to them—they were absolutely ordinary polished black shoes— but before I knew it, I was kneeling on the floor. One shoe was heavier than the other, so I tilted it and a bundle fell out. It was a man's handkerchief and inside was an opal ring and a familiar diamond brooch.

It felt like an eternity before Lord Chasterly and Simon returned from what proved to be a fishing expedition, during which I placed a few phone calls, paced the floor, and tossed back a swallow of whiskey for courage. I'd have loved to join Toni on the patio for a Blue Moon, but I was too keyed up.

At last they stomped into the house, chatting jovially. They'd caught several large specimens which were sent to the kitchen for our dinner.

I waited until Freddy had a chance to clean up, then waylaid him in the hall. "May I speak to you, my lord?"

He gave me a meaningful look. "Is it about the thing?"

I nodded.

"Best talk in my study. This way."

I followed him through the dim hall to the back of the house. His study was a masculine thing, wood-paneled and filled with leather furniture. It smelled not unpleasantly of pipe tobacco.

"Now what's this all about?" he asked.

I placed the bundle on his desk and undid the knots, laying the kerchief flat. In the sunlight streaming from the window, Mary's ring glowed softly. Freddy picked up the brooch which glittered temptingly.

"Ah, what's this? Antique. Excellent quality diamonds. It must be worth several hundred quid. Where did it come from?" He placed it gently on the desk.

"It's mine, actually. I wore it the first two nights after I arrived, and I haven't seen it since. I'm relieved to have found it. And I'm sure Mary will be glad to get her ring back," I said.

"Yes, indeed. Where did you find them?"

I glanced over at him, but his gaze was on the ring still lying on the kerchief.

"Mr. Malburn's room."

He started. "Alex? I'd have never guessed! But surely he can't have murdered Frain."

"No, of course not," I said, reaching out to smooth down a corner of the handkerchief. "The thief had a partner, and it was this partner who killed Frain."

"But I though Frain was the thief."

"Not at all. He was totally innocent."

"But why kill him then?"

"To throw us off the scent, of course. And also because he'd seen something. Something that might lead to the thieves getting caught." I was totally guessing on that one, but it made sense.

"So, they got rid of the only witness and pinned it on him at the same time. How clever," he marveled.

"Yes," I agreed. "It was."

"I suppose we must call the police at once. We may not know who his partner is, but I'm sure Alex will crack easily enough under interrogation. You can be sure I'll give you a glowing recommendation to Woodward."

"That's very thoughtful," I murmured. "Except Alex is neither a thief nor a killer."

Freddy blinked. "But you found the stolen goods in his room. He must be involved."

"Must he?" I said. "I don't think so. It was clever, hiding the items in his room. Likely another event would have happened. Another theft discovered. Possibly during the upcoming party on Saturday. The police would be called, and they would find these in Alex's room. He'd be arrested, and the partners would go about their business as before, free as birds."

"If it's as you say, then that's ghastly! But who could the real culprits be?"

"Why you, of course, Lord Chasterly."

He stared at me a moment, then burst into a braying guffaw. "Woodward never told me you had such a sense of humor."

"That's because I'm not joking. You see, you had a great idea, framing Raymond and Alex, but there were two problems."

"This should be good. What were these supposed problems?" He crossed his arms.

"The first was telling me Raymond was broke. I found the proof that he actually had plenty of money, which removed his motivation entirely."

He shifted uneasily. "Proof? I'd like to see this proof."

"I bet you would. But I'm not about to let you destroy evidence. Which leads me to your second mistake. You wrapped the goods in your own handkerchief." I removed the ring and held up the square of cloth. "The other day when I returned from the village, it had been raining and I was completely wet. Penny gave me one of your handkerchiefs to dry my face. She assured me I shouldn't worry. You had a whole stack of them, all identical. All just like this. Very unique. She said a woman in the village did the embroidery for you." I fingered the edges with their neat little stitches.

"That doesn't prove anything," he snarled, his face going an ugly red.

"Actually, I think the police will disagree with you. Especially when they search the house and find other stolen items."

His expression told me I was right.

"Don't worry. Simon will get what's coming to him, too."

He hesitated. "You've no proof Simon was involved."

"Simon has no alibi. In fact, instead of being in London during that first robbery, he was a mere twenty minutes away. In fact—"

"In fact, if you don't shut your mouth, I'll blow your ugly American head off," Mary said from behind me.

I whirled to find her pointing a little pearl handled dueling pistol right at my chest. I froze. It might be small, but I'd no doubt it would do the job. Especially at so close a range.

"I should have known it was you," I said, feeling suddenly quite stupid.

She sneered. "And how's that?"

"It was the Lanvin perfume. Everything else was stolen so it could eventually be sold off for cash, but the perfume you took simply because you liked it. It's sitting right up there on your dresser."

"It was rather stupid of you to take it, dear girl," Freddy said.

"Shut it, Fred," she sniped.

"Simon was protecting you, wasn't he?" I said. "That first night, he knew what you planned to do, and he was worried, so he drove out there to make sure you were all right."

"Stupid git. I told him I didn't need his help." She grimaced. "Everything was all planned out."

"Did he write the threat on Lil's wall?" I asked.

"No, that was Freddy. Just like it was his idea to bring in a private dick to throw everyone off the scent. How stupid could you be?"

"You know I only agreed to it because old Jamie promised to send a woman. I figured she'd be a nincompoop." He defended himself in the most chauvinistic way possible.

Mary shot him a glare. "I swear... it was going swimmingly until these idiots started having big ideas." She cocked the gun. "Too bad you'll have to die. I was getting used to you, even if you are American."

"You won't get away with this," I told her, ignoring the insult.

She laughed. "The police already think Frain was the thief. We'll just tell them when we discovered you were his partner, you tried to shoot us. Freddy fought with you and the gun went off." She shrugged. "Oops."

"The police will never believe you had to kill *two* people in self-defense," I pointed out.

"Why not?" Freddy asked. "After all, you're both criminals. And one of you a foreigner. Meanwhile, we're respectable peers of the realm. No one will ever believe we're involved."

"Why are you involved?" I asked, stalling. Maybe if I kept them talking long enough, I'd be able to figure a way out of this. "As you said, you're both respectable people with titles and money. Why would you steal?"

"Because the war devastated the economy and my own holdings," Freddy said. "I was on the verge of losing everything. Meanwhile all these imbeciles were wandering around, dripping in diamonds like nothing had ever happened."

"You figured you'd liberate a few. Save your family home," I mused.

"Sure. Why not?" Mary said, stepping around me to tuck her arm through his. "He doesn't deserve to lose this beautiful place."

"Ah." A light went off. "And you helped him because you're in love with him." Or she wanted to be Lady Chasterly, more likely.

She gave me a sly smile. "We figured stealing our own stuff now and then would throw everyone off."

"And since you were at every party, it made things easy. No one would suspect you. The parties Freddy didn't attend, he could help from the outside, taking away your haul so you wouldn't get caught."

She tittered. "We had everything covered."

"'Til that idiot Frain saw you sneaking into Lil's room," Freddy snarled, shooting her a glare.

In that moment, I realized that while Mary might have hopes of becoming Lady Chasterly, Freddy had no plans to make her so.

He was, however, happy to use her to his own ends. I could almost feel sorry for Mary. Almost.

"Yes, he really had to go. Fortunately, I was able to take care of things. Like I always do," Mary said, completely ignorant of Freddy's true feelings or my realization. She scowled at me, raised the gun, and pointed it straight at my heart. "I'm afraid, Miss Nosey Parker, you have to go too."

And there I was, standing in the crosshairs of a dueling pistol. I really do know how to get myself into the worst possible situations.

Freddy let out a yelp, and we all glanced down to find Tippy's jaw clamped around his ankle. Mary's aim wavered, her attention on Tippy who was now growling. Something exploded. Mary dropped to the floor. Porcelain shards rained down. And there standing behind Freddy—who was still trying to shake Tippy off—was Toni, arms upraised.

Freddy lunged for her, but I dove to the floor and scooped up Mary's gun. "Stop!" I fired.

A Death in Devon

Chapter 13

"Sugar!" Jack raced into the room followed by two uniformed policemen, only to stop short, staring at the scene with his mouth open. "What the devil?"

"Apparently, I'm a terrible shot." I gave him a wan smile as he gently took the gun from me.

My aim had been off, and the bullet had plowed into the doorframe instead of Freddy. Despite his being a very bad man, I was relieved. I really didn't want someone's death on my conscience.

"Would you get this damned dog off me?" Freddy snarled.

"Language!" Jack barked. "There are ladies present."

Which was hilarious, if you ask me. The man had just confessed to being involved in theft and murder. I doubted he cared about his language.

"Tippy." I snapped my fingers. "Tippy, let go."

Tippy growled around a mouthful of ankle. His blue/gray glare fixed on me as if to say, *"See what I've done for you?"*

"Yes, yes. It was very good of you to save me," I said as if talking to a dog was perfectly normal. "I owe you a juicy bone. Now will you please let go of him so the nice policeman can arrest him?"

Tippy let go, albeit with great reluctance.

"That thing should be put down," Freddy snarled as one of the policemen cuffed him.

Tippy snarled back, in no mood for his nonsense. For once he and I were in perfect agreement.

Mary was just coming to, moaning and whimpering. The second policeman hoisted her to her feet and cuffed her as well.

"Hey! What's the idea?" she snapped. "Do you know who I am? I'm innocent. Innocent, I tell you!"

Jack sneered. "Tell that to the judge."

Good grief, it was like I was in a Hollywood detective flick. I turned to Toni. "How did you know I was in trouble?"

She sank down into one of the leather club chairs, looking a little pale and shaken. "I was coming in to fetch another Blue Moon when I saw Mary crossing the hall with a gun in her hand. I knew she couldn't be up to any good, so I followed her. When I saw her waving that thing at you... well, there was a very large vase in the hall."

"You hit her over the head?" Jack said, horrified. "What if she'd shot Sugar?"

"Well, that wasn't going to happen, was it?" she snapped back. "I waited until Tippy distracted her."

"Speaking of. How did this little guy know I was in trouble?" And why would he bother to save me? Wasn't like he cared much for me. Or anyone else that I could tell.

I knelt down to give him a pat on the head. He took it with good grace.

"I have no idea," Toni admitted, "but as I was looking for a weapon, he came rushing out of nowhere straight for the study. It was like he *knew*." She eyed him closely. "You don't think he's psychic, do you?"

Jack's laugh turned into a cough. I barely managed to keep a straight face. Tippy just looked haughty and majestic.

"Thanks, Jack, for running to the rescue."

He winked. "Any time, Sugar."

I ignored the blush that threatened to rise. "What will happen to Mary and Freddy now?"

"They'll be arrested and locked up. There'll be a hearing. And eventually... well, justice will be served." Jack shook his head. "Uncle is going to be horrified when he hears it was Lord Chasterly behind this the whole time. I don't understand why he'd hire my uncle in the first place."

"He never expected him, or rather me, to be able to solve anything." I said. I did not mention that Freddy had called me a nincompoop.

"Probably another red herring," Toni said, getting up and rummaging through the cabinet against the back wall. The rich wood matched the desk.

"Toni, why did you tell me Alex doesn't have money?" I asked.

"He doesn't." Her head was so far into the cupboard, her voice came out muffled.

"But I found a big wad of cash in his room."

She pulled her head out of the cupboard and shot me a grin. "Oh, that. He probably won."

I frowned. "Won?"

"Oh, yes." She turned back to her rummaging. "He's an inveterate gambler. Quite good at it, too. When he bothers. Or when he cheats." She shot me a wink. "How do you think he affords those fancy togs?"

I guess that explained it. I felt relief Toni hadn't lied.

"Aha! Anyone?" She held up a crystal decanter filled with amber liquid.

"I could use it," Jack said.

"I suppose," I said, not particularly enthusiastic. I didn't care for straight up liquor, but I was feeling oddly shaken.

As if he sensed it, Jack steered me toward the second club chair. "Here, have a seat. You've been through a shock."

"Tippy! There you are, you naughty pooch." Penny popped through the doorway. "Sorry Miss, but he got away from me. I've been looking everywhere. I hope he hasn't disturbed you."

"Not at all. He just saved my life."

It took some time to get accustomed to my new life at Aunt Euphegenia's cottage. Fortunately, Mr. Woodward said I could donate whatever of her personal things I didn't want to a local charity, which I promptly did.

With my own clothes in the closet, I felt a little more at home. I even discovered that my aunt had been a collector of detective novels which gave me plenty to read in the evening. I was starting to think Aunt Euphegenia was a woman after my own heart.

I did mention to Mr. Woodward, strongly, that I didn't appreciate being manipulated. I mean, of course, his claim of the cottage having a sea view. Surprisingly, he apologized and assured me he would never do that again. A week later a nice seascape watercolor arrived. It went perfectly above the grate in lieu of the heavy oil painting of daisies that had hung there.

Walks with Tippy down by the sea had become the highlight of my day, and we went rain or shine. Mama wrote me at least once a week—she still wasn't thrilled I was staying in England—giving me an excuse to venture out to the post office for a chat with Mrs. Johnson. Tippy and I had settled into a routine that more or less satisfied both of us.

Mr. Woodward had been thrilled with my investigations and had sent me a bonus with my paycheck. Jack had visited twice. "Just to make sure you're okay," he said. I had a feeling it was more than that but didn't want to rush anything.

I also discovered I was now stuck between my feuding neighbors, Mrs. Druthers and Mr. Carbuncle. No one seemed to recall how the feud had started, but whatever it was, it must have been a doozy. Their verbal sparring was monumental. One afternoon they annoyed me so much, a pail of cold water "accidentally" made its way onto Mr. Carbuncle's pajama-clad form.

Lil had been cleared of all wrongdoing which I was glad about. Her jewelry had been found locked away in Lord Chasterly's bedroom and returned to her. She'd written me a note of thanks which was elegant and stiff at the same time, but I forgave her. Lil was a prickly sort. She'd warm up to me.

Alex went off to Monaco to gamble, or so Toni informed me.

"To cheat at cards again?" I imagined him dressed in a tuxedo and making all the ladies swoon.

"No doubt," she laughed. "I swear that man likes to live dangerously."

Toni and I had become friends, which surprised me. We wrote each other frequently and I'd even visited her in London a couple of times where she'd dragged me around to plays and nightclubs.

The fate of Endmere and its staff was, unfortunately, still unresolved. Lord Chasterly was being forced to sell in order to cover legal expenses—although I had no doubt they'd find him guilty no matter how good a barrister he found. In the meantime, the staff was staying on to run the place. I hoped whoever bought it kept them on. Even cranky-pants Johnson.

It was an overcast morning when the phone shrilled. It hadn't rung the entire time I'd been living there. Both Tippy and I stared at it with misgiving. At last I answered on the fifth ring.

"Hello?"

"Miss Martin, pack your bags," Mr. Woodward ordered without preamble, voice muffled and staticky down the line. "I've another job for you."

After a brief conversation, I hung up. Propping my chin in my hand, I eyeballed e dog. "You know, Tippy, a woman's work is never done."

Tippy gave me a haughty look and wandered into the kitchen in search of treats.

My stomach rumbled, letting me know that it, too, would like a treat. I stood up and followed him. "For a dog, you really do have the best ideas."

The End

A Death in Devon

Shéa MacLeod

Coming in Fall 2019

A Grave Gala

Sugar Martin Vintage Cozy
Mysteries – Book Two

A Death in Devon

Shéa MacLeod

Sign up for updates on Sugar Martin:
https://www.subscribepage.com/cozymystery
In the meantime, check out the Lady Rample Mysteries, set in glamorous 1930s London, beginning with *Lady Rample Steps Out*.

A Death in Devon

Shéa MacLeod

Note from the Author

Thank you for reading. If you enjoyed this book, I'd appreciate it if you'd help others find it so they can enjoy it too.

Lend it: Feel free to share this book with your friends!

Review it: Let other potential readers know what you liked or didn't like about the story.

Sign Up: Join in on the fun on Shéa's email list: https://www.subscribepage.com/cozymystery

Book updates can be found at www.sheamacleod.com

A Death in Devon

About Shéa MacLeod

Shéa MacLeod is the author of the popular cozy mystery series, Lady Rample Mysteries, as well as the award nominated Viola Roberts Cozy Mysteries. She has dreamed of writing novels since before she could hold a crayon. She totally blames her mother.

She resides in the leafy green hills outside Portland, Oregon where she indulges in her fondness for strong coffee, Ancient Aliens reruns, lemon curd, and dragons. She can usually be found at her desk dreaming of ways to kill people (or vampires). Fictionally speaking, of course.

A Death in Devon

Other books by Shéa MacLeod

<u>Sugar Martin Vintage Cozy Mysteries</u>
A Death in Devon
A Grave Gala (Coming Fall of 2019)
<u>Lady Rample Mysteries</u>
Lady Rample Steps Out
Lady Rample Spies a Clue
Lady Rample and the Silver Screen
Lady Rample Sits In
Lady Rample and the Ghost of Christmas Past
Lady Rample and Cupid's Kiss
Lady Rample and the Mysterious Mr. Singh
Lady Rample and the Haunted Manor (Coming Fall of 2019)
<u>Viola Roberts Cozy Mysteries</u>
The Corpse in the Cabana
The Stiff in the Study
The Poison in the Pudding
The Body in the Bathtub
The Venom in the Valentine
The Remains in the Rectory
The Death in the Drink
<u>Witchblood Mysteries</u>
Spells and Sigils (Coming August 2019)
<u>Intergalactic Investigations</u>
Infinite Justice
A Rage of Angels
<u>Notting Hill Diaries</u>
Kissing Frogs
Kiss Me, Chloe

Kiss Me, Stupid
Kissing Mr. Darcy
<u>Cupcake Goddess Novelettes</u>
Be Careful What You Wish For
Nothing Tastes As Good
Soulfully Sweet
A Stich in Time
<u>Dragon Wars</u>
Dragon Warrior
Dragon Lord
Dragon Goddess
Green Witch
Dragon Corps
Dragon Mage
Dragon's Angel
Dragon Wars- Three Complete Novels Boxed Set
Dragon Wars 2 – Three Complete Novels Boxed Set
<u>Sunwalker Saga</u>
Kissed by Darkness
Kissed by Fire
Kissed by Smoke
Kissed by Moonlight
Kissed by Ice
Kissed by Blood
Kissed by Destiny
<u>Sunwalker Saga: Soulshifter Trilogy</u>
Fearless
Haunted
Soulshifter

Made in United States
Troutdale, OR
06/24/2025